One affair
Two couples
One God
One believer
One unbeliever
Two adulterers
One cuckold
One woman scorned
Many sins

A NOTE ON THE BOOK

Forgive Us Our Trespasses is a dark and passionate work on human nature under the influence of love, religion and secrecy...

Hannah and Alex meet by chance, but perhaps inevitably. A passionate love affair consumes them, and threatens to destroy their married lives, their beliefs, and perhaps even themselves.

Often startling imagery portrays their physical and mental states as the affair grips them. Its effect on each of them is profoundly different, creating a startling juxtaposition of thoughts and beliefs. But their fates are entwined until the end, leading to a deeply resonant and thrilling climax.

A NOTE ON THE AUTHOR

Emily Hunter grew up near Bath. She has two science degrees but also loves literature and writing. She now lives in London spending her free time reading, writing, travelling and taking photographs. This is her first published novel.

Forgive Us Our Trespasses

EMILY HUNTER

BLUE MARK BOOKS

First published in Great Britain by
Blue Mark Books Limited in 2015

This paperback edition published by
Blue Mark Books Limited in 2015

www.bluemarkbooks.com

A catalogue record for this book is
available from the British Library

ISBN 978-1-910369-08-1

Blue Mark Books Limited supports the Forest Stewardship Council®. The
FSC® promotes the responsible management of the world's forests.
All our books carrying the FSC® logo are printed on FSC®-certified paper

MIX
Paper from
responsible sources
FSC® C013604

Typeset in Adobe Caslon Pro by
Blue Mark Books Limited

Printed and bound by
CPI Group (UK) Ltd, CR0 4YY

"More tears are shed over prayers answered than ever there were over prayers unanswered."

St Teresa of Ávila

Fireworks

Him

No one need tell me to remember, remember, the fifth of November, for that was when I first saw her.

I was walking home from work, down the dark High Street, past the Ring O'Bells, a comforting glow behind its curtained windows, and onto North Lane. Some fireworks cracked from a nearby garden, shrill as the exclamations of the children watching them, and showers of red sparks appeared over the chimneys of the cottage standing between the apparent gathering and me. The rasping whisper of a rocket ascending became audible as it cleared the rooftop, followed shortly by a low but thunderous boom, which surprised me in its volume, though I knew it was imminent. Thousands of tiny stars radiated from the point where the noise had sprung, like the beginning of the universe, though these stars faded and died within seconds of their inception.

The sound of quadrupedal pawsteps brought my eyes down from the heavens, and met those, wide-eyed and terrified, of a Border Collie trotting towards me, tail firmly clamped between hind legs. Crouching, I intercepted it, grabbing its collar. The tail wagged, half heartedly and rather apologetically, but he was clearly pleased to have found me. I offered some words of comfort, and ruffled his coat and patted him. This pleased him, and his shaking subsided. Beneath his collar dangled a tag which read *Little Cottage, Henry Lane*.

Henry Lane was one of prettiest, and by night, darkest roads in the village, and one that I had not yet explored thoroughly. But the moon – waxing gibbous – was out and it was a fine, crisp evening. The dog was obedient, despite his fear, and he followed me when I bade him, though he kept his head low and his tail down. I walked and he trotted. We passed the painted cast-iron road sign of Henry Lane; it was rendered almost illegible by black-leafed ivy which had crept up the limestone wall upon which the lettering had been placed.

Little Cottage was easily found; its name was proudly displayed in black lettering on the white-painted wooden garden gate, at home between the low front walls. A little stone path ran up to the door of the aptly named home. The Collie sniffed the gateposts, perhaps hoping to find evidence of unwanted visitors. His ears pricked and his tail extricated itself from between those hind legs as we heard voices from within the cottage. The gate creaked open and clattered closed behind us once we had passed.

I could find no knocker or bell, so rapped my knuckles on the door. The excited exclamations of children came from the hall and the Collie looked at me, head cocked and tail almost wagging.

Then the door began to open.

I first noticed the knuckles and fingers of a beautifully proportioned female hand grasping the back of the lock, and as the door swung open, as my aperture into this cottage – this household – widened, the person opening the door came not into sight, but hid herself behind the portal enabling two small children to occupy the fore. The children – a boy and girl – aged maybe five and seven respectively had such expectant faces, which changed to joy as they simultaneously cried, 'Benji!' that I broke into a smile immediately.

I looked down and noticed the modest booted foot of the woman who had opened the door. The boots, low-heeled and of dark brown suede, were well worn; the suede had in part been polished shiny by the hem of the jeans resting on them. My eyes followed the legs upwards, past the trousered calves and wonderful thighs, evident even beneath trousers. By now, the door was almost fully ajar; I knew her gaze followed the children and that she was smiling, but my eyes were still stuck on her belt. It was of beautiful red-brown leather and had a beaten brass buckle now polished smooth by wear – perhaps it had been her father's or grandfather's – it had, noticeably, but not obviously, been worn by someone of considerably greater girth than her. And I noticed something else, some imperceptible hesitation, something.

We watched the children playfully admonish Benji, and I became aware with a sense of slight dread that we'd not made eye contact, despite what must have been several seconds elapsing since she'd opened the door. I looked up, past the v-neck jumper and white shirt beneath, past a tiny vestige of cleavage evident between open buttons, past the protuberant clavicles, adorned by a few strands of brown – no, not just brown, but chestnut, auburn, burnt sienna – hair which had escaped from being tied back with the rest. Past the slim neck and elfin chin until I found her eyes.

What eyes!

We were both still smiling from watching the children, who, now, retreated with Benji into the warmth of the hall. Our faces remained the same, our eyes locked, for what seemed like too long, neither of us seemingly to know what to say.

I saw her bright, dark irises – small as her pupils were large – and her white, white whites, shining; the slight wrinkles at the corners of those eyes, happy wrinkles, wise wrinkles; the small, but ennobling bump on her otherwise straight nose; the way the individual hairs of her eyebrows created such a beautiful, unadulterated shape; the cheek bones, high and defined; the soft, modest lips and tiny vertical crescent moons of smile lines, in action at the corners of those lips, her lips.

Then her smile changed. The physical variation of her features was scarcely perceptible – indeed I believe she tried not to exhibit any vacillation – but her eyes gave her away. I hoped her smile was no longer for the children and that instead she smiled at me. But as we continued to say nothing, her smile began to fade, in acknowledgement, perhaps, that something between us had already happened. As she uncrossed and re-crossed her legs to shift the weight from one to the other, to put that which had been behind in front, her smile relapsed further into a half-smile, an almost quizzical smile, emphasised by a tiny unbelieving shake of her head. The children had now withdrawn further into the cottage, and their voices were muffled; my sense that this unforced silence had continued for too long became more urgent, though the silence was destroyed not by either of us speaking, but by blood pounding through my ears. Her smile, like mine, had almost totally regressed, her crescent moons becoming almost straight, like longbows being relaxed, except that the less tension there were on them, the more built up between us.

But the tension snapped, almost audibly, as we simultaneously broke into smiles again. It had to happen; we had already crossed the line. Hers was wonderful, broader and livelier than before, and unequivocally for me. I dared to believe it was a glorious admission of her attraction to me. Was it attraction? If not, certainly intrigue.

Something – I think a thought of hers – broke the spell we had found ourselves in, and she spoke.

'I'm Hannah.'

Her voice, like her face, seemed immediately beautiful.

Those two small words told me that she was confident but not arrogant; that she was kind, and happy; that she was firm, yet submissive. And her choice of words made my heart jump: she hadn't thanked me for bringing Benji home, she hadn't greeted me, or bid me good evening, she hadn't said anything to begin a conversation. She had said *I'm Hannah*, at once presenting herself to me, offering me a little piece of her being and intriguing me to want to know everything about her. And she had done it on purpose.

I told her my name.

'You look like an Alex,' she said. 'Why are you smiling?'

I had known what she was thinking.

She smiled, recognising this to be true.

'Benji... Thank you. It was the fireworks,' she explained, unnecessarily.

'It was a pleasure.'

'I haven't seen you before – are you new?'

I couldn't help it – I smiled again – this time because of the wording of her question, as if I was inferior, or unwanted, because – as I explained – I was – we were – indeed, new to the village.

'Well,' she said, 'I'm sure I'll see you again, then.'

'I hope so.'

This was my cue to leave, although I sensed hesitation and unwillingness in both of us. I tore my eyes from her, and retraced my steps down the dark garden path, partially lit by the light emanating from within the cottage but obscured by Hannah's body. Now with my back to her, our shadows merged. I knew her gaze followed me, and every part of my body burned. I took none of my surroundings in; I could only envisage her smile, the creases at the corners of her eyes, her ear lobes, unpierced.

I turned towards her, to say goodbye, for now at least, and stepped back straight into the low, closed, garden gate.

Forced Inevitability

Her

It was only when he crashed into the gate that I really knew.

I had come back to the village I knew and loved, after university, after London, with my childhood sweetheart, Edward, now my husband, and father of my children, thinking that I had been lucky in love, and that the part of my life where temptation would or could have tempted me was long past. But now, Alex, Alex, an avatar of the Devil had presented himself on my very own doorstep. On the limestone slab that Edward had found and fashioned and set. I never thought the Devil could be so beautiful.

I spent that night awake, dreaming of him.

Him

It was a month before I saw her again.

My nights had been turned into sleepless fantasies, my days into dreams. Whenever I left my house, I hoped to see her in the village, perhaps walking Benji, perhaps with the children. I went to the Post Office, regularly, using any excuse, to buy a pint of milk, to buy stamps, to post something. Even the beautiful blonde girl, Anna, whom I came to learn spent even more time there than me, talking to the ancient Postmaster, interested me not in the least. But after a month of such pointless wanderings, on a Saturday, I decided that I would have to force events further.

And so to Henry Lane, on a fine frosty December day, the weak sunlight lifting my mood, but providing no warmth, not even to melt the frost encrusted on spider's webs aguising the hedgerows. I came to the sign of Henry Lane again. In the daylight, the ivy appeared less black, though the leaves were the deep green of last summer's growth. In places, the aerial roots had weakened the loose lime mortar between the limestone blocks of the wall, and now some of the mortar hung from the ivy, loose and redundant, and its gnarled trunk probed deep in the crevices that the mortar had once occupied. The leaves still obscured the lettering of the sign, though the quality of the casting was still evident, despite the flaking paint, and ferric red streaks running from sore welts of decay.

Henry Lane itself was glistening white with frost, and slippery as a result. I picked my way carefully up it, treading on the darker areas of tarmac which afforded more grip. Little Cottage came into sight, and my heart raced when I saw Benji, panting, billowing clouds of warm doggy breath into the cold air. He saw me coming, and, wagging his tail, jumped up at the gate, letting his forepaws fall between the upright timbers which formed crenellations along its top surface. Benji's battlements; would he let me pass?

The racing of my heart turned to a definite pounding when the noise of Benji lolloping on the gate caused Hannah to straighten up from a crouched position, behind the wall which had previously hidden her. She was alone.

Her

I had been scared to see him again. But see him again I knew I would, and needed to, in order to rid my mind of some terrible thoughts and temptations.

But seeing him again only worsened my turmoil. This initial greeting was a disaster. He'd come up to the gate, eyes fixed on me, and rested his hand on the gatepost, while with the other he patted Benji's head and grabbed his ears playfully. He wasn't interested in Benji though. He didn't even look at him. He only looked at me. Our faces were solemn, as mine should have been. I prayed Edward wasn't looking out of a window. Any onlooker could only have drawn one conclusion. As before, the sensual tension was eventually broken by our simultaneous smiles, and then I asked God to disallow Edward to see, because those smiles were more telling than our previous solemnity. My guilt for asking Him to intervene in such a situation was immediate, but did not stop a wonderful sensation of excitement and happiness coming over me. I cursed the Devil, or God, I don't know which, for allowing it. I hadn't had such a wave of emotion crash into my heart since I'd first made love with Edward on our nuptial night.

'Morning,' he said gaily, as if he was just a friendly neighbour.

'Morning,' I replied, suspiciously. Suspiciously enough for him to notice? Yes. His smile dropped. I had to make it normal, before my control of the situation was lost. Before I said or did something which would allow events to unfold despite my own free will.

'Settling into the village well?' I asked. It worked. His slight frown relaxed.

'Yes, we – that is, my wife, Kitty, and I – are enjoying life in the country. We were in London before.'

'Yes, likewise… but I grew up here.'

'In this cottage?'

'No, the Vicarage. My father was the vicar.'

'Retired?'

'Dead.'

'I'm sorry.'

I smiled. He didn't need to be sorry.

'It must have been a wonderful place to grow up,' he said, unabashed.

'It was. It is.' I paused. 'It was.'

He smiled. I wasn't sure he understood. The rest of the conversation was just as stilted and as forced. We both knew. Neither of us knew, though, how social graces worked under these circumstances. Perhaps they didn't. It didn't surprise me that he had found me again. It didn't surprise me when, quite without thinking about it, I'd asked him – and his wife – to our Christmas drinks party. Though I knew why he'd walked up our road, there was no other foreseeable conclusion to our meeting.

Social Fraternising

Her

I had been looking forward to our annual drinks party. Everyone in the village came. Young parents, their children, and old parishioners alike. Now my emotions were mixed. Because he was coming, every time I thought of it, my heartbeat quickened and my excitement grew. I began counting down the days until I would see him again, like Lucy and Harry with their advent calendars. But I was terrified. I was no actress. Would Edward see? Would his wife notice?

On the day itself, I was busy preparing. There were nibbles to make, cleaning to be done, and as always, the kids to keep entertained. Each Christmas seemed to get more exciting for them. How lovely it was to see their faces, rosy and happy in anticipation of the big day, but how tiring! But I didn't get short-tempered with them.

For the first time, perhaps for years, childlike excitement was creeping into my bones the nearer it got to six o'clock, the appointed hour for our party. I understood how the children were feeling. But the business of the day kept my thoughts at bay, and preparations went almost as they always had done, me doing the food, the kids helping to do the easier bits, and Edward making the fire and preparing the glasses and mulled wine. Except this time I made more effort with everything, just so that things would be perfect for *his* arrival.

By the time the guests had started to arrive, I was hanging on every rap on the door. Every time I was disappointed when one of my friends, or villagers arrived. When would he come?

Him

For the second time, I rapped on her door, *their* door perhaps, but this time, it was in the company of my wife. A wry smile crossed my face at the thought.

The door opened but my delighted smile faded when Hannah was not standing there, as she should have been. I knew this was her husband; who else could he have been? Of course I knew she was married; I had seen her wedding ring, and of course the children were hers, but my fanciful imagination had invented other scenarios to explain away these profoundly obvious realities.

Edward, as he turned out to be, introduced himself, and asked whether I was the saviour of Benji, welcoming me, us, when I admitted I was. I introduced myself, and Kitty, all the time looking over this impostor's shoulder for a glimpse of *her*. Edward started telling us how glad he was we could come, and how pleased he was that his wife was so good at inviting new friends.

New friends?

The oddity of this remark was still reverberating around my head as we entered the house, and went through the hallway, towards a busy-sounding living room where those whom had already arrived had congregated and were chatting. Kitty, always a little shy, prompted me to enter after Edward's lead, so I did. As I entered the room, I felt as if every pair of eyes in the room was clapped on me, suspiciously analysing my motives. In fact, of all the thirty or so there, only the couple nearest the door turned, and then without much interest as they saw it was no one they knew. Their conversation continued and my eyes flicked from one face to the next, desperately trying to find her.

Edward said that she, without using her name, was putting the kids to bed and would be down shortly; he introduced us to another couple of our generation. He offered us some mulled wine, the alcoholic fumes of which made me cough slightly as I inhaled them, and the five of us stood talking. Normally a social creature, this evening I found myself in no mood to make polite conversation with these folk, least of all Edward, who had already married Hannah. On the mantelpiece, I noticed a picture of the family, on a beach, Hannah's body tantalisingly wrapped in a wet sarong, at once revealing and hiding her covered curves to me. I tried not to look at it. The guests gradually circulated: further introductions to people that weren't her. I tried hard to level my eyes with those in our immediate group, but failed: I looked over the heads of women, and between the heads of men, searching for her, for a glimpse of her at least; and having found neither, my eyes then continually sought out the entrances to the room, one at each interior corner, but she did not come. When I did catch the eyes of those faceless guests, they were empty; I did not engage with them; I did not listen to their questions, not caring whether my responses were what they had expected, not listening to the answers they gave to Kitty's queries. I cannot remember their names. I was there only in body, and that body and the whole of my soul cared for one thing alone – and that thing could enter at any moment.

Her

I saw his wife first. I knew it was her. Her beauty matched his. She was talking animatedly with Edward and my heart sank. I didn't want our spouses to like each other. Everything would be so much harder.

When I had entered, I had desperately sought him out from my other guests and found him quickly after his wife. From that moment on, I always knew where he was in the room though I dared not look straight at him. And when I eventually I did, he was looking at me. His expression didn't change once our eyes had locked, and I don't think mine did either. Hearing the woman next to me say my own name snapped me out of my trance, and despite the huge urge to the contrary, I couldn't bear to glance his way again.

Of course, I spent the first half hour talking to everyone except him and his wife, but Edward asked me if I'd said hello yet, and invited them to join the little group I was then talking to. Kitty, she was called, was delightful. She had to be! Edward and she did most of the talking, while we tried to avoid each other's gaze lest we gave ourselves away. I couldn't concentrate, and remember little of the conversation. It was only when he spoke to me alone that his words embedded themselves in my memory forever. I was glad when my role as hostess forced me away from the group to bid farewell to the doctor and his wife, old friends and longstanding churchgoers.

After their departure, the small talk of my remaining guests began to annoy me. Didn't they know I no longer had time for such trifles? I wanted only to talk to him. To unbutton his shirt, and run my hand across his broad chest. To put my face near his. Stop! Too much mulled wine. What arms, though... I began to imagine them enveloping me, but Edward's voice shattered the image unkindly.

Would I like some more mulled wine?

Is that all he wanted?

But I did want some more.

He smiled kindly, pouring my drink, spilling a large drop on the carpet.

That afternoon I had scrubbed that very carpet, after Harry had walked in mud from outside. I scolded Edward, unfairly, for his carelessness. His expression became sad as my knit eyebrows and fierce eyes shot him an angry look. But I couldn't stop myself. Guilt racked me, but I couldn't apologise. What was happening to me? I was cross with Edward. He didn't seem to be able to leave me alone just for a moment. A moment on my own with Alex, just a moment was all I needed... It seemed as though Edward was suspicious already. I knew he wasn't. It was the guilt. Why does guilt play so with the imagination?

I went to the kitchen for a rag for the wine. Alex came in, alone.

'We must be going.'

'We've hardly seen each other.'

'It's difficult.'

The first vocal admission had been his. Did this count for anything? But he was alone. Did I know what I was about to do?

Him

'After Christmas,' she said. 'Can you come over on the first Tuesday in January?'

'Yes I think so.'

'I'll be waiting.'

'What time?'

'Eleven.'

'Morning?'

She nodded.

She was so proper, so wholesome, I could hardly believe she'd said it. I could decide not to go, but I knew I wouldn't. There was no turning back now. Since meeting Kitty, I'd never so much as looked at another woman, and now here I was agreeing to see this Hannah, this unknown, but bewitching creature, not in sordid London or some other metropolis, but in a sleepy English village, not the setting for such a meeting, but perfect a stage nevertheless.

But now I had to wait.

The Waiting Game

Her

What had I done?

Waiting for the drinks party had been hard. Now I was being tortured. But I was my own torturer. I had begun this. But it was more than just torture. Excitement vied with guilt as my prominent emotion, and often won. This though would increase my guilt, only for it to be overtaken again by excitement. Thus my thoughts ran wherever they led me, preventing me from sleep.

But it wasn't just these thoughts, either. The guilt separated itself into three. The most obvious cause was Edward. I'd loved him entirely for years, and now he seemed empty and redundant. But he was always there. I had to sleep with him. I wanted to push him away, and on occasion felt myself doing so. I tried not to, but it was difficult. It was difficult. It was.

Then there was my father. What would he think? Could he see my actions or read my thoughts? Previously, I'd taken comfort in believing he could. Now I hoped he wouldn't. My father had been vicar of the parish throughout my formative years, but he was needed by God in another place. God took him without warning, in his sleep, with one heart attack, a kind way to take him, a death fit for one whom had served Him his whole life.

And thoughts of my father entwined themselves with thoughts of God himself. If my father couldn't see my thoughts, or chose not to (but why would he do that?), God could. I began to pray, to ask for forgiveness for things that hadn't yet passed. Things I knew I would do. But this wasn't right. This wasn't what Jesus had taught us. And so my thoughts ran back to my father. What would he think of this radical type of prayer? What would

Edward think? Edward, who now seemed to spend hours and hours asleep next to me, innocent of my evil thoughts. My father used to tell me to think healthily; that my mental life would in time reflect that of my physical existence. Sometimes, I wished it would. Sometimes, I couldn't help wishing my depraved thoughts would come true. Sometimes, these thoughts would almost make me reach out to Edward just to satisfy a need.

But Edward wasn't that need, and so my thoughts went round and round, day after day, each day of waiting getting longer and more wearisome. Dear Edward didn't even seem to notice how tired I had become. Sleep came to him easily, and so did arising. Sleep eluded me, and once I had found it, I hated losing it. I forced myself to wake and dress and get on with the day.

And then a fourth source of guilt began to emerge. I had initially banished thoughts of Lucy and Harry. My children were not part of this. But as I became more tired, so my temper shortened, and their little misdemeanours made me cross beyond their significance.

By Christmas Eve, I was exhausted. My body performed all the preparations, and other necessities of the day before the birth of our Saviour, but my thoughts were elsewhere. Edward had fallen asleep reading in bed. I was so tired that after I'd removed the book from his flaccid fingers and placed his Christmas stocking by his lifeless lump, I slept immediately.

On Christmas Day, in church, I almost fell asleep in the sermon.

Almost.

Him

I don't know what made her turn round at that moment – perhaps it was that feeling that someone had been watching her. Someone had. It had been hard not to stare at the back of her head right from the beginning of the service, but as the vicar's voice droned on and on, so my thoughts wandered further and further from his tedious preaching. She was wearing her hair up, and I began to imagine undoing the hairclips holding it in place, letting it fall over her shoulders, running my fingers down her elegant neck to those wonderful clavicles; and then her shirt buttons, the clasp at her back, setting her free.

When she turned round, I went stiff. I wanted to glance at Kitty to see if she had noticed, but couldn't. Hannah smiled, briefly, guiltily, touched her hair, or nearly touched it, through nervousness, and that was it: she turned away.

It was electrifying.

The sermon seemed to finish very quickly after that, although afterwards, when we arose for the Nicene Creed, I noticed the pew had made my bottom numb.

Kitty had been surprised when I had suggested we went to Church. But, I had told her, the run-up to Christmas had been so busy: visiting our old friends in London, drinks parties in Town, last minute shopping in the chaos of Oxford Street, Regent Street, Jermyn Street for shirts, port, cheese, amid the choking fumes of red buses and black cabs. It would be nice to take in the atmosphere of the village church, I had said, the serenity, the calm. And indeed, it would be a good chance to make new friends. She had vocalised her worry that they would all be Christians, but I in turn had pointed out that not everyone who went to church, especially in a village, was; she agreed, and so we went.

I didn't find it as disagreeable as I was expecting, although in truth I hardly took anything in, except her. After the service, we departed rapidly in order to make it for Christmas lunch at Kitty's parents. I didn't even get near enough to say hello, but she did give me a little wave, and Edward smiled at us. She looked tired.

And so Christmas came and went, a happy time, despite everything. Kitty was pleased to have seen her parents, and we went to a New Year's Eve party in London, again clutching onto fragments of our old lives in order to make the transition into country life less abrupt, less different. Neither of us had come from London, so leaving was a decision that wrenched us from our friends, our jobs, our first house, but not our roots. The friends, we reckoned, were the biggest loss, but we believed the move would be worth it. We didn't want to bring up our planned children in London, and we would have a spare room for those friends who fancied a weekend in the country. Our old friends had no idea how mesmerising a sleepy village could be, and I smiled at the irony of some of their comments. They had never expected us to leave London.

Yet leave we did, and on New Year's Day I felt pleased to be leaving again, and to be coming home this time, pleased to be away from the bustle and temptations of the city. We went for a walk on the hills. The air was clear, and we saw for miles. Kitty stopped me at a kissing gate, and demanded a kiss; she looked wonderful, her cheeks rosy in the cold wind, and for a moment, I hardly thought of Hannah. But as I put my hand on the gatepost, I felt leaves, and glancing down, I saw ivy, dark green: last summer's growth. It hadn't grown since, but, I thought, it would start again in the spring, and its coils would soon leave the gatepost, seeking out the sapling that grew next door.

I kissed Kitty at that gate, and, being on holiday, made love with her more than usual over that weekend. But my eyes were closed, and I thought not of her blonde hair, but of brown hair. No, not just brown, but chestnut, auburn, burnt sienna.

And after the weekend, routines started their grinding motions again: people began returning to work, and I noticed new routines, normal commonplace routines, but routines which had now become more relevant in my life: the Lent term started; playgroups opened; children disappeared for the day. But the more normal these routines appeared, the more scared I became that the abnormal would descend upon my life before too long.

Union

Her

I sat in the kitchen, my heart beating double time to the ticking clock.

Eleven o'clock struck.

My heart quickened.

It was close to thumping its way out of my chest when I heard a knock.

I stood up and breathed hard, trying to compose myself. I found myself at the front door as if in a dream, and saw my hand reach out to the lock. This was only the second time I'd opened the door to him. What did he expect? Without wanting or being able to think further, I opened the door.

He stood there, breaking into a smile as our eyes met. It was a kind smile. He looked kind. But how could he be kind if he was here? But I had asked him here, and I was kind. So it was all right. But I had never done this before. Had he? Was this normal for him? How could I tell him these things? If I relayed my fears before anything had happened, perhaps it would kill the flames. I needed this fire. I needed this man.

'Hello,' he said, thankfully breaking my thoughts.

'Come in.'

He did. I closed the door, and we stood facing each other.

He smiled again. Kindly. Was he nervous? How could he smile like that if he was nervous?

'I'm not sure what to say,' he said. He was nervous! But what a way to declare it!

'No,' I said. 'It's difficult.'

'Yes,' he said, understanding.

It didn't look like he had thought of anything to say, and I began to relax a little, though I was still wary and almost shaking with excitement and fear. His face had engraved itself into my mind the moment I had seen him and I was pleased it hadn't changed. He opened his mouth to speak, but nothing came out, and he closed it again. It reminded me of a goldfish, and I smiled at the thought, looking down to avoid questions. When I looked up again, it was clear he was waiting to speak again, so I let him.

'If I didn't think it was entirely wrong, or not what you wanted, I'd kiss you.'

So I kissed him.

Just softly at first, my lips barely touching his. It was the only part of our bodies that touched and yet I could feel bolts of lightning running right down my arms and legs. My eyes were closed. I could feel his breath and smell his skin. Our lips still touched. But soon I wanted more. As I pressed harder, the edges of our mouths met. He put a hand, very gently, on my hip and I found his other with one of mine. I began to feel very light-headed, and steadied myself by placing my other hand on his chest. Maybe he was feeling the same, because this caused him to fall back against the closed front door, parting our lips. My eyes sprung open and found his. He was all right. His lips were slightly parted and I knew what they wanted. I stepped forward and without thinking about it, curled a hand round his neck, and placed one of my legs tightly between his. His lips opened a little wider.

I don't know how long we spent up against the door, but my hair felt pretty tousled by the end. It was uncomfortable, though, and not how I'd envisaged things.

We'd only kissed.

The damage was repairable. Wasn't it?

But still I wanted more.

'Come upstairs?'

He nodded.

I knew the enormity of these two words, *come upstairs*, but I did not dare think about their repercussions, so I didn't.

Back to now.

I didn't want to turn my back to him, so started ascending the stairs backwards, my hand still round his neck. I tripped and fell and flushed in embarrassment, but his hand deftly found the small of my back and he raised me to my feet as if he were righting an empty wine bottle. What strength! He was much more strongly built than Edward and I began to want desperately to his feel his weight on me. I could feel my body react to this want.

I led him to the bedroom.

Although I'd taken down mine and Edward's wedding photograph, this was still our room. It was where our children had been conceived. It was very odd bringing Alex, an almost total stranger, into it.

My nerves returned.

He kissed me.

My nerves dissipated, as did my reserve.

I spent the rest of the afternoon changing sheets and sewing buttons back on.

Him

She had asked me to make to love to her, but I could not. Since we were married, I had only turned down such an offer from Kitty a handful of times, and even then she usually won by unfairly stripping, or whispering what she would like to do to me in my ear.

But tonight I simply could not; I was spent. Kitty became petulant, and asked me why, only gaining her sympathy when I said I thought I must be coming down with something, since it was most unlike me.

I did not tell her my illness was love.

After a while, Kitty drifted off to sleep, and my imagination led me into Hannah's arms.

It was comfortable there; it had been comfortable there. But the comfort only came after the passion. It still amazed me she had been as she had been: I had not expected her to pin me against her own front door, nor that leg to hold me there; a staircase had never been a scene for love, but now, even ascending my own earlier that evening, I had felt her hand around my neck, and I had smiled, remembering her fall, which made my blundering into her gate less painful to recall; I had not considered that someone could be so beautiful, so bewitching, so... the words escape me; I had not thought anyone could writhe so perfectly in time to my movements, under me, next to me, around me.

I was aroused. I knew I would not be able to sleep for two reasons, and so woke Kitty, saying I was feeling better; but she was too tired now, and fell asleep again, almost immediately.

Back to Hannah.

I couldn't quite believe I had ripped open her blouse; I had never done that before, not even with Kitty. I had enjoyed it, and she had not cared; her blouse was not damaged, only buttonless: we had inspected it, afterwards, as I had inspected her, once her blouse lay on the floor. Her sheets had been in a mess when I left, and I wondered how she would cope.

Carrying On

Her

'I told him I wasn't feeling well, and that I'd spent the afternoon in bed. I told him I'd spilled a cup of tea. I did actually spill some tea, so I didn't have to lie. It was all right to do it once, but I can't keep making excuses. We'll have to be more careful.'

'What are you going to tell him this time?'

I looked down.

'Bugger.'

The sheets were in a worse state this time. Then it dawned on me I had sworn, and I flushed.

Of course he had come again. I didn't have to try hard to make him do so. He wanted me as much as I wanted him and all I'd had to say was, 'Next week?' and he'd nodded. The week without him had flown past and it seemed so natural that he was here again.

It had gone quickly because I was so happy.

My happiness sprung from how he made me feel. I felt as if I was the most important thing in his world. I think I was, then. It contrasted so profoundly with Edward, who seemed to think about everything else, except me. I knew this wasn't true, and that he loved me, in a way, but not in the way Alex did. Alex worshipped my body. Seeing a full-grown man in awe of how I looked was something unknown to me. My ego hadn't been complimented like this before. It was touching too. I touched my own collarbone, remembering his gentle fingers running over it. I touched my lips, remembering how his felt on them. In the mornings and evenings while changing in or out of my bedclothes, I touched other parts of me, remembering the way he had done the same. Sometimes, whilst doing mundane chores, I imagined his breath on my neck. The hairs there reacted as if he had breathed on them.

I was happy by day at least.

At night, when not thinking of Alex, I was tormented by ever increasing, nauseating pangs of guilt. His second coming had been so easy. 'Next week?' I'd asked. He'd nodded. My words and his response echoed, unendingly. It felt terrible that it was so easy. Just two more little words. I wouldn't make it so easy this time. I couldn't. I didn't want to be his mistress. But I knew as soon as he'd gone, I'd be yearning for him again.

As so often before, I had prayed to my dead father. I hoped he'd understand. He'd always told me to follow my passions, but did this count? Had he ever been tempted in this way? I doubted it. As a vicar, his faith must have been strong enough to withstand temptations of the flesh. Temptations presented by the Devil. But what about my faith? Was I worthy? I thought again of how I had prayed to God, asking Him to forgive my sins before I'd committed them. I prayed again, asking him to forgive the sins I now had committed, and for forgiveness for that sinful prayer.

I felt better once I had done so. God had forgiven me. But still I longed for Alex, and I became worried about any thoughts that ran through my head. Or my heart. And my heart seemed almost to give me away. Memories of Edward asking what I was smiling about haunted me. 'I was miles away,' I had said, elusively. He hadn't probed me.

But now Alex was here, in my bed, I didn't think about any of the unhappy contemplations that wore me down in his absence. I felt safe in his arms. They wrapped me up and shielded me from these thoughts.

And hours with him passed as if they were minutes. It seemed so unfair that time should run so. Just when I wanted the moment never to end, end it had to. Paradoxically, I didn't want the unruly January sun to set. It meant he had to go, and Edward and the kids would arrive home.

'I'd better be going,' he said, as if reading my mind.

'Yes,' I said unenthusiastically.

I wanted to tell him I loved him. I did love him. Love at first sight? Impossible? I had once thought so. Edward had to persuade me to kiss him, all those years ago, and he'd asked me to marry him three times. Third time lucky, he was. Alex could've asked once, and I'd have said yes. It was ridiculous. I was so in love that although I hardly knew him, I couldn't think of anything he could do to change my feelings for him. He seemed so perfect, physically and temperamentally.

He rose from the bed, flicking back the covers. I watched his muscles working as he crossed the room to where his clothes lay, scattered on the floor. I didn't want him to dress. It was marvellous watching his lithe lines. When he buttoned his trousers, I thought of undoing them again. His shirt now covered his chest, but I could imagine running my hands over it.

Now he looked at me.

I felt self-conscious as he looked at my chest. It wasn't fair that he should look on me, when he was now clothed.

I picked up my blouse which had, though I have no memory of it, been thrown over my bedside table. My Bible lay there, and we both looked at it, each acknowledging its presence, and each other doing so.

Him

She had seen me notice that mysterious tome, that fictitious volume, that book which has caused so much harm through the centuries, and today. Those holy, prophetic, God-inspired, or, as some believed, God-written words, open to endless interpretations depending on the state of mind or education of the reader. Her expression asked me to explain.

'You don't believe all that nonsense, do you?'

'I'm a vicar's daughter.'

'Oh.'

'I love you,' she said.

It did not surprise me that she had said it, but I noted her timing.

'I love you too,' I said. I knew it was true, and it did not surprise me that I had declared it. I knew from the moment I saw her that I would love her. It was the way we met that brought me back to her, last time, and now again. Kitty and I had been friends before we were lovers; there had been no great meeting, no immediate and overwhelming attraction. There had been no such meeting with anyone before Kitty; I had not thought it possible anyone could meet like that, in such a fateful and unexpected, yet natural manner; it seemed unreal, but yet so real that I knew I could not bear not to pursue it. Maybe that is why she said she loved me then. Maybe she could not bear not to pursue me, but did not want to pursue an unbeliever, and so silenced me. At that moment, I did not care, and threw off my clothes again, joining her on the bed; I wanted to feel her naked chest on mine, just once more, and pulled her blouse, which she had been covering herself with, away. I found her mouth with mine, and her naked skin up against me, all down my body, right to her feet, which were tucked under the arches of my own.

But we both knew time that afternoon was running out.

'Things are going to be a hectic next week,' she said. 'I'm not sure when I'll be able to see you again.'

I started panicking; surely she could not be thinking of ending it all after only two visits, just a few hours of bliss, just after we had said we loved each other? Maybe falling in love with me scared her; maybe she had not meant to, and could not cope; would the lies be too much? Would God forgive her? Was she thinking that? What *was* she thinking about?

'Darling, I do want to see you again,' she said.

Church

It was Kitty who suggested we went to church again, and I agreed, though not too hastily.

We stepped out into the cold and wet; normally, I would have used such conditions as an excuse to stay in, light a fire, read, and be cosy in front of it. But despite the rain, I was happy. I knew she would be there. The umbrella quickly turned inside out, and Kitty, usually much more hardy than I, became annoyed. Not I. Naked trees danced in the wind, and shook drops of water larger than the raindrops over us, just as Hannah's hair had done in the shower. Kitty became further vexed.

We were rather damp when we arrived, but thankfully the church was warmed by the archaic heating system, amazingly still going. I mused that its longevity might have been God wishing to keep his house warm, but that it was more likely to be a result of fine Victorian engineering and because it was used only once a week. The church smelt of damp coats and mouse shit, that smell so subtle, you do not really notice it, yet know exactly what it is.

Silence reigned as the frocked priest emerged from the vestry and solemnly walked down the chancel, pompously waiting far too long for the silence that had already come, before announcing a long list of tedious notices. Kitty looked at me when I sighed, and whispered that I had better get used to it, meaning, I think, that village life would be like this. I smiled to smooth her doubts, and furrowed brow, but also because I knew village life would be fine: just not when it revolved around the Church.

This being the second time in church in quick succession after a long cessation of ecclesiastical attendance, the rigmarole of the service began to pall quickly. The sermon was just as bad as the one at Christmas, full of non-explanations, non-sequiturs and teaching so illogical I wondered if the vicar knew what he was saying, or had thought about what he was saying since theological college, when so many stock words and phrases seem to be imprinted indelibly on the minds of the clergy for them to regurgitate unthinkingly upon the expectant masses. It did seem, however, that the vicar had at least taken the trouble to amend a previous homily to include current events of particular concern to him.

His uninspiring words and flat voice caused my thoughts to wander. Hannah and her family were sitting in the same pew as they had been before. Were they such regular churchgoers that they had their own pew? I shrugged this thought off as Hannah had shrugged off her buttonless blouse.

Kitty brought me back into the proceedings by tugging on my shoulder; I was the only member of the congregation still seated. Thus the flock stood for the Nicene Creed, to tell the world what they believed. Nothing changed. The flock still bleated the same words: '*We believe in one God…*' and I stood there in silence, wondering at the blindness of these otherwise perfectly normal, educated, sentient beings. I said the only bit I felt I could. '*In accordance with the Scriptures, he ascended into heaven…*' It was true, the Scriptures had, in some way, promised it, so I didn't mind saying it. It was just a shame that the Scriptures were so wildly misguided. I began to become angry that the woman with whom I had fallen in love believed all this nonsense.

This time after Church, we stayed for coffee.

It was served in cheap little cups, the size of large thimbles, and most of my coffee was in the saucer, but I did not mind because it gave me an excuse to see her, the only person besides Kitty that I knew in the village.

Edward, of course, was there; he seemed to cling to her like a limpet, though I knew this was unfair: perhaps she thought Kitty clung to me in a similar manner. It wasn't long before the four of us stood in a circle talking about how rotten the weather was. The weather! The weather was the last thing on my mind, and I resented our spouses being present; if they hadn't been, Hannah wouldn't have been saying how damp she was, and how she wished she were at home: we would be naked, in bed, expressing our emotions not through tedious, pointless meteorological observations, but through our bodies, in union, as we had before.

Hannah introduced us to the doctor and his wife, whom we had seen, but not spoken to at the Christmas drinks party. He was called Parsons, a thoroughly unsuitable name for a doctor, I thought, but an amiable chat followed before they took their leave.

Kitty said how charming they both were.

'Yes, but I'm not sure why they come to church,' said Hannah.

Kitty asked what she had meant.

'I don't think they believe in God. They come because it's traditional. I find it hypocritical, don't you?' asked Hannah, directing the question at Kitty alone.

Kitty said nothing, disagreeing.

Edward tried to lead the conversation onto less controversial topics, and his wife scowled at him; he looked a little frightened. I wondered whether this conversation would begin again once they were home.

Several friendly members of the congregation, and the vicar himself, introduced themselves, asking how long we'd been in the village, where we had come from, and all those other questions one asks in such a situation.

They were all very welcoming, especially the vicar, no doubt wishing to expand the size of his flock at every opportunity. Despite this perhaps cynical thought, I was struck by all their kindnesses and began to feel, for the first time since I had left my parents' own little village, part of the community. It was a good feeling, it was why we had left London, and I thought that perhaps it was a reason for coming to church again.

The coffee cups were being collected and the parishioners

were donning their damp coats as the open church doors allowed God's Sunday hot air to be exchanged with his miserable, cold, January firmament.

'We should go, darling,' said Hannah.

Darling?

Last time I had heard use that word, she had said it to me.

Kitty too wanted to leave; she was cold.

And so we braced ourselves for the wind and rain and headed for the door, where the vicar stood, blessing his congregation as they left. Who was he to bless them, this old, ignorant, deluded man of the cloth?

Still, I had to shake his hand, and thank him; but for what I was unclear.

And so into the porch, where the wind was blowing in the rain making it quite as wet as the churchyard beyond. Deep puddles had gathered in the worn flagstones under the porch, and several umbrellas which had been leaning against the wall had fallen into them, drowned and sodden.

The rain was relentless, and the four of us raced for the roofed cover of the Lych Gate at the edge of the walled churchyard, pausing momentarily in the respite from the deluge to say goodbye before we headed our separate ways. After this brief farewell, Edward and Kitty were the first to depart, their hooded faces cowering from the driving rain, and although Hannah and I followed our respective spouses almost immediately, the slight pause allowed her to mouth two words at me.

Tomorrow.

Eleven.

Postponement

Her

At five to eleven I heard a knock on the door.

He was early, and I hadn't quite finished changing the sheets. Edward and I had only changed them yesterday, hurriedly, just before Church, and I couldn't risk having them on the bed today. I had found some ghastly sheets we'd never used, a wedding present from one of Edward's aunts, and decided to put them on, temporarily for Alex's visit. Now the bed was made half in each set, and I was annoyed that he'd come early because I didn't want him to come up to this scene of tedious domesticity.

Then something strange happened.

After the knock came the jangle of keys, and after that the unmistakable sound of a key entering the lock, and then the lock turning. I was frightened.

Alex did not have a key. Did he? Had he taken one? Had he got one cut? Anger flashed through my mind at his undoubted impudence. But no, surely not? A burglar could quite easily have done the same. A burglar could have appropriated a skeleton key. Skeleton key. The phrase struck a chill for a moment into my heart. Harry had a toy skeleton key for opening padlocks. As a mother, I had encouraged his fascination of learning, though I had been concerned that his toy opened many of the simple locks about the house. If a toy could do that, a professional could do much worse, and I was a woman, alone. But Alex would be coming. I began to hope he would arrive early to stave off any attempts the burglar might have on our belongings, or me. But then the most obvious, though in my mind the least likely, scenario presented itself.

Edward.

Him

Kitty was always enthusiastic in bed. She was also beautiful. It was what every man would have wished for in a wife, though for me, that morning, I just wanted to be left alone. She had other ideas and her persistence reminded me of a phrase that a womanising acquaintance had once said, which at the time annoyed me greatly, and made me acknowledge he was a cad: 'The thing about good-looking women is that *someone* is always bored of fucking them.'

But being Kitty, she got what she wanted, though I was tired, and thinking only of Hannah.

I had spent the night in fitful sleep, dreaming. Hannah's words had echoed round my mind, and around my bedroom.

Tomorrow.

Eleven.

In my semi-conscious state in the cold, dark small hours, I began to fear Kitty would hear her, and I said, 'Darling, I know, I am coming.'

Kitty had whispered sweet words to stop my dream, and I had fallen asleep again only to believe I was already there, lying in Hannah's arms.

'Darling,' I had whispered, again, reaching out for Hannah, and finding Kitty, whose voice brought me again back to reality.

Thus the night passed, and so to that Monday morning, Kitty arousing me, and satisfying herself, leaving me spent and unsatisfied.

Kitty soon dressed and departed.

After washing almost as carefully as Lady Macbeth, I had breakfast.

Her

Could it really be Edward?

It could be him; he was the most obvious candidate. But he'd only left a couple of hours before and wasn't due back until after he'd finished work that evening. Fears of Alex, and burglars, and

31

again Edward shot through my mind as I dashed silently to the top of the stairs where I could see the door opening at the end of the hall below.

It *was* Edward!

I was physically safe, at least, and the fear of unwanted men vanished instantly, leaving a momentary, ironic taste. But this latter thought never properly materialised as the realisation of the appalling situation I was now in struck me.

'Darling! What on earth are you doing home?' I asked, breathlessly.

Edward told me I had better not get too close.

My heart pounded louder than before, and I fancied he could hear it. Did he know? *I had better not get too close.* He must know. He was revolted by me. By my behaviour. He must know. He had come home to have it out with me. To confront Alex when he arrived.

'Darling! What on earth do you mean?' I managed to say, without thinking more, desperately wanting a quick and rational answer not to do with Alex, and hoping that the tremor in my voice had been noticeable to only me.

He said he felt terrible.

Was he torturing me on purpose?

He looked up at me with sad eyes, and must have seen my expression of horror and doubt, because his mouth relaxed slightly into a smile. A sad smile, but a smile nonetheless. Was it a wry smile? A smile of acknowledgement that our lives together were over?

'Darling, for God's sake, tell me what the matter is!' I said, in a croaking whisper. My throat was dry, and a lump there stopped my words forming normally.

He was ill.

He had a sudden fever.

He had been sent home.

Thank God!

My relief was enormous, but I realised my initial reaction to his homecoming had been odd and flustered, and I must carry this on, in mock concern, until I was sure he was all right. Guilt hit me as I realised that only a few weeks ago, I would have wished his illness could have been passed miraculously to me so that I could bear his suffering and pain for him. To take away his discomfort because I loved him. Not now. But something must be said.

'Oh, Darling, I am sorry!' I said descending the stairs. 'Come into the kitchen and have a hot drink.'

He thought he needed to lie down.

The sheets! How would I explain the sheets? We'd never used the ones that now half made up the bed... I hadn't spilt tea... Even if I had, I wouldn't have used those sheets...

I found no answers, and impressed upon him the need for a hot drink.

He seemed to agree, and to my joy headed to the kitchen, allowing me to pull out a chair for him as he sat at the table.

I put the kettle on.

He said he'd begun to feel peculiar when he'd left home, and that by the time he'd reached work, he knew he was becoming ill. An hour later he had been sweating, and his ashen face had convinced his colleagues he should be at home. And then he said he really needed to lie down.

No excuses had presented themselves to me: I just needed three or four minutes in the bedroom without him.

I'd just finished making his drink, and passing it to him, said: 'Why don't you drink this, and I'll make you another. Then you can go to bed.'

He wanted to lie down immediately.

'You can't drink lying down!' I said, almost in desperation.

He thought, maybe, that he'd go and lie on the sofa, and pottered off, drink in hand.

Thank God!

But was it God to thank, or fate?

As soon as the situation had resolved itself, another, far worse one loomed into reality as the kitchen clock struck eleven. Its ticking beat in my head, and grew louder and louder, my heart pounding, now three beats to each tick. A knock on the door would be disastrous.

Him

I left home at half past ten, intent on approaching Henry Lane and Little Cottage not from the south as I had before, but from the north, from the outskirts of the village. Suspicions from inquisitive neighbours, from behind garden walls and net curtains could be powerful in a small community, and the gossip of fellow parishioners could be disastrous; a new route would lesson the chance of these malicious rumours spreading like a malignant cancer. More importantly, I would not have to pass the sign of Henry Lane, whose constricting parasitic ivy and rusting ironmongery had of late been occupying my thoughts to an unusual degree.

Her

I quickly decided that Alex knocking on the door would be much worse than explaining the sheets, and I quickly decided that Benji needed to go to the loo, despite him sleeping peacefully when Edward had come home.

'Darling,' I said, coming into the room where Edward lay on the sofa, 'Benji's desperate. I must take him out. I won't be five minutes. You wait here, and I'll get you another drink and help you upstairs to bed soon.'

Edward compliantly nodded a sleepy agreement. He hadn't noticed Benji slumbering by the Aga, or if he had, he said nothing.

'Benji! Walkies!'

We left to find Alex, turning down the lane towards the village.

Him

I still had no real idea what I hoped or expected to come of seeing Hannah in this secret and immoral way, but I was pleased to be on the way to her house. I felt more comfortable going a different way; it felt less obvious, more as though I was just exploring the outskirts of the village. Although it was more contrived, it felt less so, as if I might stumble on Hannah's house by accident, on a walk. It felt less as though I was embarking on and enjoying an adulterous affair.

I walked up to the end of high street, which runs parallel to Henry Lane, and at about the corresponding point where I imagined the houses of Henry Lane turned into fields, I turned up a little footpath next to an old red phone box and between two houses of the high street. The path was wet and muddy, and not frequently used, judging by its state of disrepair and overgrown hedges, presumably not cut back for some months. Maybe this would be a better route in the future, I thought, though I would have to take my shoes off when I arrived because of the mud. After a hundred yards, I saw the end of the path, and the tarmac of Henry Lane beyond. Once I had come out onto the lane, I saw with mild satisfaction that my judgement had been about right, and the first houses on the outskirts of the village lay only fifty yards away. Little Cottage lay nearer the centre of the village, beyond them.

Her

Once we were twenty or thirty yards from the house, I began to breathe more easily. Alex had not yet come, and I couldn't see him down the lane.

Now all I had to was intercept him, kiss him…

Could I risk a kiss outside the confines of the house? No, someone would see. So all I had to do was intercept him and say I'd see him the same time tomorrow. No, that would never do. Edward could easily have 'flu, and he'd be in bed for days if so. Same time next week. That sounded so filthy. But I knew I'd say it, and I knew I'd look forward to it. I was cross with Edward for ruining today's liaison. It was bad enough seeing Alex without dramas like this.

I just had to intercept him quickly, and get back and put the right sheets back on the bed.

Except he didn't come.

By quarter past eleven, Benji and I were still lingering at the end of the road, and I began to get anxious. Why was he late? Maybe he couldn't get away. Maybe Kitty was ill. Was he ill? Perhaps he'd seen Edward returning. Perhaps Edward had seen him on his way back and stopped to say a friendly hello. It might have worked itself out. Then there were only the sheets to deal with...

But a horrid thought struck me.

Perhaps he'd come in the other direction up the footpath from the High Street.

Him

I knocked on the door; there was no answer.

I waited a few moments, and tried again, a little louder. Why was there no bell or knocker? With my last knock, though, the lock clicked from its latch, and the door stood ever so slightly ajar.

I smiled. Maybe this had been planned. Images of Hannah waiting for me on the bed upstairs flashed before my eyes, and my excitement of seeing her increased. I kicked off my filthy shoes and entered.

'Hello?'

Nothing.

I went through to the kitchen which was empty. The back door leading to the garden was bolted. She must be upstairs! As I went back into the hall, intent on going upstairs, my attention was caught by a tiny sound emanating from the door immediately at the bottom of the stairs.

I walked in to find Edward lying on the sofa.

Her

I'd had a brainwave, and when I arrived home, I scrawled on a piece of paper 'Not today, thank you' and stuck it to the front door. Edward would be inside all day, and if by chance he did see it, I'd say it was for the fishmonger who came round the village. It shocked me that lying was becoming so easy, but they were lies to protect Edward, not hurt him, and so I reasoned it was all right.

Then I went into see Edward who was still thankfully on the sofa.

I thought he was asleep, but my presence seemed to stir him, so I asked him softly if he wanted another drink.

He did.

I returned with one, and we sat for a minute or two on the sofa, me asking him how he felt, what he wanted, and him answering and saying how much he loved me for my kindness.

If only he knew.

I told him I was going to find some extra pillows and dashed upstairs changing the sheets as quickly and as quietly as possible, and grabbing a couple of extra pillows from the spare room, dumping the unwanted sheets in there at the same time. I stopped at the top of the stairs to compose myself, and once done, descended.

'Darling, I think you should come to bed now,' I said, helping him up, and then following him up the stairs.

'Would you like a shower to warm you up?'

He nodded.

So now, instead of undressing Alex, as I had been imagining and dreaming of, I began to help my husband to rid himself of his sweaty shirt, his body clammy and unpleasant below. I turned the shower on for it to warm up, and once it was, Edward walked in. I rolled my sleeves up, and washed his back. Once pyjamared, Edward lay back on the mass of pillows and smiled up at me. I couldn't help smiling back. I still loved him dearly, and now felt sorry that he was so ill. And he must have been very ill. His forehead was on fire. I stuck a thermometer in his mouth. He looked dreadful and had hardly said a word since he'd arrived home. The bedside clock read twenty five past eleven. If Alex was coming, he'd see the note. I concluded I was safe, and finally relaxed. Edward reached out and tenderly stroked my face, telling me he loved me by doing so.

'I love you too, darling,' I said.

I did.

I fetched some water for him.

Half past eleven.

I took the thermometer out.

'A hundred and three,' I declared. 'If you weren't so ill, I'd be very cross that you had got your shoes so muddy.'

The New Normality

Her

Edward malingered in bed for days, and much of my time was spent looking after him and the children when they were home. But in the gaps, those periods in the day when Edward slept and sweated upstairs, I thought only of Alex.

He hadn't come.

Why not?

When I had been waiting at the end of Henry Lane for him with Benji, my reasons for his non-arrival were all practical. Edward had mentioned nothing about him when he'd come home from work ill, which lead me to conclude that Alex must have seen the note on the door. Another practical reason, I concluded, and a good one.

But despite this, my imagination ran wild.

I suddenly realised that under the Lych Gate, when I'd last seen him, when I'd invited him quickly, he hadn't answered me.

Tomorrow.

Eleven.

They were the only words I'd said. Had they been enough? I hadn't even said them, only mouthed them. Had he read my lips? My only response had been a glower from under his knitted eyebrows. I'd thought the rain and cold had been the reason for his grim face, but now I doubted my judgement. Had Kitty seen? I had assumed her hood had hidden me from her eyes at the critical moment, but now I wasn't sure. Had I, in two words, destroyed their marriage? Would they destroy mine too? Was he bored with me already? Maybe he was a man who once he'd conquered, left. Perhaps he wanted to come, but couldn't face the lies. Certainly

I was getting better at them, and inventing excuses, and I began to accept that to see him, I must perfect them. The stress of that Monday had been almost too much, and left me emotionally exhausted after it. These additional worries compounded my strain. For my sanity, I had to banish all thoughts of guilt and God. I simply didn't allow them to surface.

It helped, but my thoughts ran like this for a week.

The following Sunday, Edward was well enough to come to church, and I set off in high spirits, aiming for an opportunity to ask Alex to come again. But neither Alex nor Kitty were there, and my hopes were dashed.

I went to bed that evening in confusion, fear and misery.

Him

It had been a near miss, sure enough; but I resolved to go again the next Monday, whether Edward was there or not. Despite everything, I had enjoyed the excitement of a week ago, and risks and excitement would be my new normality if I was going to continue to see Hannah. Armed with a plausible excuse, I set off for Little Cottage.

Her

It's funny how confusion, fear, and misery can be dispelled so quickly.

The next week, he had come.

'What the hell are you doing here?' I had said angrily as I'd opened the door.

'What the hell was Edward doing here last week?'

I shouldn't have been angry; he had a right to be. But how did he know?

'I take it you're alone?' he'd asked.

'Yes.'

He had kissed me passionately, and I had kissed him back.

He had come.

Now we lay in each other's arms.

I was blissfully happy.

Edward had never made me feel like this. Edward didn't make me feel so secure and so wanted. Now, in Alex's arms, I wanted to sleep. But I couldn't. I mustn't. A new fear of falling asleep until Edward returned to find us, naked, stopped me. But the desire was there.

'So what *did* happen last week?'

Alex's question stopped my thoughts.

'Edward came home from work, ill. He had a really high temperature.'

'I wondered what he was doing on the sofa.'

'You *saw* him?'

'I walked in on him.'

Terror struck me. What had they said? Why hadn't Edward said a word. He must know, now, surely?

'He was asleep,' said Alex, smiling.

Why was he smiling? Did he think this was some game? This was my husband. My marriage. My life.

'Alex! I can't cope!'

And I couldn't.

I rolled over, out of his arms, away from him.

I cried.

'I'm sorry, darling,' said Alex, 'but all's well that ends well.'

'No, all is *not* well! How can this carry on?'

'The chances of such a near miss are so remote, I'm not scared of it happening again!' he said gaily. I wondered if he enjoyed it, like a character from a film might. Like James Bond might.

'The chances of something happening on any given occasion are no less, simply because they've happened before,' I pointed out, remembering the words of a maths teacher from years ago.

My thought that the power of human recollection is extraordinary gave way to anger when Alex said, 'Oh, Hannah! You're so serious sometimes!'

I turned to him. My expression told him how I felt.

But I needed to know more. Events were so confused that

I couldn't imagine that they had possibly worked out without Edward becoming suspicious, or worse. What had he done when confronted by my sleeping husband? How had he got in? How had he left? I asked him.

'The door came open when I knocked.'

'You knocked?'

'He was asleep,' said Alex, presumably to reassure me, but instead filling me with worry. 'I went in, thinking you'd be alone. But you didn't answer when I called, so I looked around.'

'You called for me?'

'Yes, just before I walked in on him. He was sound asleep.'

'Are you sure?'

'Quite.'

'How?'

'I said hello to him.'

'You did *what*?'

'I said hello to him. No one in their right mind would have feigned sleep.'

I began to wonder if he was in his right mind. And then again I became angry at the thought of him treating our affair – our *affair* – as a game.

'What would you have done if he'd been awake?'

'I would have thought of something.'

'Is this all just a game to you?'

'No. Please calm down.'

'What happened then?' I asked, so that I wouldn't become more irate.

'That's when I heard the garden gate slam. I crossed the hall into the dining room, and hid behind the door.'

He was evidently enjoying the story.

I became angrier.

'I think you are enjoying your game,' I said.

'Of course not. Look, you would know if he knew, right?'

'I think I would…'

I knew I would. Edward couldn't have kept this to himself. It would destroy him, and he wouldn't be able to keep that from me.

'Good. That's when you got home,' continued Alex. 'Where were you anyway?'

I explained.

He had come down the lane from the other end.

'Well,' he continued, 'I heard most of what happened next, and slipped out when the shower was on. I thought I'd be pretty safe. Your bedroom overlooks the garden. He couldn't have seen, and the noise of the front door clicking shut wouldn't have been audible over the shower.'

'Yes, I suppose…'

'So I picked up my shoes and walked out as quickly as I could without even putting them on. Then I tried not to hurry so as not to raise suspicion from your neighbours.'

'They were *your* shoes?'

'Yes!'

'I didn't think I recognised them… my mind was in such a whirl.' I paused. The dreadful thought had entered my mind a split second before my mouth had formed the word, 'Shit.'

'What?'

He looked concerned.

He should be concerned.

'I told Edward that if he weren't so ill, I'd be cross about how dirty his shoes were.'

He looked more concerned.

'Won't he be suspicious?'

The question didn't seem as if it needed asking or answering.

But then I remembered Edward, later in the week, cleaning a pair of particularly dirty shoes. My worry began to ease.

'I think it's all right. I think he did actually have a pair of dirty shoes.'

'Sounds all right, then,' Alex said, perhaps hoping to convince himself as well as me.

'Yes,' I agreed, perhaps doing the same. 'So you didn't see the note?'

'No. What note?'

'Of course you didn't. I put a note on the door saying "Not today thank you," but you were already inside.'

'What would you have said if Edward had seen it?'

'I would have thought of something.'

'Is this all just a game to you?' smiled Alex.

I tried to stop myself, but couldn't.

I smiled.

The thought of Alex wandering along a wet country lane carrying his shoes made my smile broaden. The fact that he'd even thought about how quickly to walk whilst carrying his shoes made me laugh.

'What?' he said, apparently irked by not being included.

'How did you think carrying your shoes would not raise suspicions from my neighbours?'

'I would have thought of something!'

We laughed.

It was extraordinary that things had worked out as they had.

We had to laugh, I suppose, to keep sane.

I pulled him closer and wrapped his arms around me again. He seemed to have a knack of making bad situations all right.

But now Alex was here, though he had extinguished my anguish and anger, and I lay happily with him, more doubts began to creep into my mind. I thought how peculiar it is that once your biggest worry vanishes, a new one, one that head previously been lurking in the depths of your mind, comes to the fore, to eat away at your soul, your being. And I feared even Alex would not be able to allay this worry. It had started the night before when in my sorry condition I hadn't been able to sleep. So many thoughts revisited my mind and circulated there without conclusion that it hadn't surprised me that this one should eventually surface.

Edward had noticed I wasn't sleeping, and as he'd done when we were first married, he'd wrapped his arms around me from behind. But I'd felt trapped, not safe as before. Only Alex made me feel safe now. Edward had soon fallen asleep, as he always did, and his weight had begun to lean on me more heavily. It had felt like he was squashing my lungs, and I'd suddenly realised I'd needed air, so slipped out of his clutches and sat on the edge of the bed, gasping. Relieved to be free.

Free of him, but not from God.

I had switched on my bedside light.

Edward still slept.

I knew I was on the verge of thinking this important but unwanted thought. Letting it come into my head, to go round and round without ever deciding what to do about it.

I had almost picked up my Bible. I often did this before bed, or on waking. Sometimes I would read a passage I knew. Sometimes I let the book fall open, hoping that God would choose which words I needed to read that day. It made me wonder whether choosing whether I would open the book in the New or Old Testament, or even in the Gospels, where the edges of the pages were more worn that the rest, was a function of me hoping to find some words I wanted to read, or whether it was God, helping me to find what He wanted me to read.

But that night, the Bible had remained closed.

I knew there was nothing in it that could mend my new fear.

My new regret.

Alex was an unbeliever.

Why did God bring him to me? An unbeliever. This avatar of the Devil. I had prayed to God, asking him to tell me why. To show me. The result had only been wild, immoral behaviour. Behaviour that I didn't think I would ever exhibit to my husband, let alone another man. I felt a surge of blood rising to my face, just I had felt so many other physical and emotional surges since Alex had arrived.

I remembered him looking at me.

'What are you thinking?' he'd asked.

'Just how you make me feel.'

It hadn't been a lie. It explained my embarrassed face.

'You are beautiful,' he'd said.

'As are you, darling.'

'I wonder how many people feel like I do when I see you?'

'I think I do.'

We smiled.

Joy lifted up my heart, as nothing had ever done before, and so thoughts of God were banished, and we didn't talk about it.

But he must have known it was on my mind. The Bible. My response to his question about it. All that nonsense, he'd said. How cruel of him. But he didn't know he was being cruel, unlike me. I'd been rude and confrontational to him and Kitty in Church. In God's own house. And I'd done it on purpose, to belittle him, after he'd belittled the Bible. But maybe all I had done was insult Kitty and embarrassed us all. Would God forgive me? I had, in a way, been defending Him. I prayed quickly and silently but felt nothing. Perhaps God did not answer the prayers of an adulteress when she was in the arms of her lover. Perhaps He was punishing me.

I felt as if I was being punished when he had left.

And so it carried on.

We carried on.

He had come, and he came again. Soon, his weekly visits became my new normality. Our new normality.

The bed had become ours by day. Indeed, we hardly spent any time anywhere else. By night, I lay there with my husband, but my heart was with him.

But now Alex was here, and I felt happy.

'Do you feel guilty?' he asked. Even though he'd been with me an hour or more, these were the first words he'd said.

'It's getting easier.' It was. 'Do you?'

'No. It feels like the right thing to do.'

How could this be the right thing to do? We were both married. We had both made promises before God. I was, as we lay there, breaking a promise to God. The thought terrified me, and if I hadn't been in his arms, I would've leapt up, and begun to pace the room. But I didn't. I was in his arms. It did seem like the right thing to do.

'Yes,' I said, not telling him my previous thoughts. There were so many doubts in my mind, that to have vocalised even one more seemed too much to cope with. I knew it would be pointless, anyway.

Even though we'd been seeing each other regularly, there never seemed to be enough time. When Alex arrived, we hardly spoke until after our desires had been met, and then it was almost time to part. And so little conversations began, but were never really finished. There was no great desire to finish them. We both knew that we were on borrowed time. Time borrowed from our spouses, and our other lives. Talking about these stolen moments only wasted them.

But I began to want more than just his body. His body. My mind was stuck there. His body lay behind me, and I could feel his warmth, all down my back and beyond to where our legs were intertwined and our feet lay together. We fitted together well. I looked down at his strong hand reaching over my side, cupping one of my breasts. His fingers were long enough to hold it in its entirety. It brought warmth to my heart. Perhaps directly, I mused. His wrist too was strong, but slender, and I followed his forearm, vanishing under my own arm. Though now relaxed and passive, when he lifted me, or manipulated me to make our connection yet more perfect, the muscles in it danced, each one almost visibly working beneath his skin. Then I imagined the muscles in his upper arm doing the same, bulging as they worked. I loved holding him there, and feeling them, as I felt him inside me.

I sighed at the thought, and he stroked the hair out of my face, raising his head slightly to look at my face.

He reacted so well to my thoughts and needs.

I craned my neck to face him, and found his lips again, now turning my body towards him as I felt him stirring.

We made love again.

Even though I had begun to want more than his body, I hardly dared think about where our paths were heading. It frightened me. It had bigger implications for me. I had children. But I began to realised that we couldn't continue this indefinitely, though it suited me well. The village was small. People might begin to notice. I might leave something undone in our bedroom. Our bedroom. It was mine and Alex's now, but in a few hours, Edward would believe it to be mine and his. The thought of Edward trying to become intimate with me revolted me, and I buried my face in Alex's armpit. It smelt, but it smelt of him, and I loved it.

'Do you still fuck Edward?'

'Only when I have to.'

I paused, not knowing what to say. I began to feel as though I had said the wrong thing, but despite everything, I tried not to lie. I'd never lied to Edward. I'd just omitted the truth.

'Edward repulses me sometimes.'

His eyes found mine. Was he surprised?

'Do you sleep with Kitty?' I had asked it, but I didn't want to hear the answer.

'Yes. I sometimes think of you.'

Sometimes?

The answer stung, but she was beautiful. I knew it would be hard to think of me unless he closed his eyes.

I think my expression gave me away.

'It's hard,' he began. 'We've always enjoyed each other… regularly, I mean… so it would be odd for me to suddenly stop. She might become suspicious.'

His reasoning began to mend my wound. He was a man. It was different for him. But it still hurt.

And I did begin to want more than his body, whatever that meant for our combined, and separate lives.

'I want to do something different next time,' I said.

The Walk

Him

She had wanted to do something different, so we did.

We had arranged to meet outside the village, to go for walk along the scarp slope of the hills overlooking it, the same place that Kitty and I had walked a few weeks earlier. I too was pleased to be doing something other than arriving at hers, despite the excitement that Little Cottage now seemed to bring.

I was waiting at the stile. I knew which one she had meant: it was made of a single slab of limestone standing upright and set within one of the handsome dry stone walls that were so characteristic of the area. The Levels were set out below, like a huge patchwork quilt, little hedges being the seams between the patches of fields, stretching for miles, some areas glistening with winter floodwater, and every now and then a small hillock rising above the flat boggy fields, much greener and dryer. Up here, it was dry; the soil was thin and overlay the jointed, porous limestone bedrock.

For the second time, Benji's pawsteps alerted me to his presence, and I looked down the road to see him and Hannah walking up.

'Hello, this is a surprise!' she said, approaching happily.

It did not amuse me, but the sight of her striding powerfully up the hill towards me made me smile. Her smile broadened and I became slightly irked that she had misinterpreted me; how funny that such a small thing should cross my mind. I knew I would never be able to explain every little thought like that to her; my mind worked too quickly. But now, I thought, we would finally have some time to talk, to get to know each other, not simply satisfying our carnal needs, though this last did concern me. I wanted her badly.

She had almost reached me.

She looked gorgeous: her hair was largely tied back, though little strands had come loose, or had been deliberately left hanging over her face; I wanted to stroke them to one side, to see her eyes more clearly, but then let them fall back in place, imperfectly perfect. Her chest heaved as I had seen it do before, but this time it was from the exertion of climbing the hill; but still, images of it bare flashed before my eyes, and made me catch my breath. Her jeans, covering those athletic thighs, were splattered with mud, and she didn't care – I could tell she didn't care – and then I wondered what she was thinking.

'What are you thinking?'

'About you. Your body. You?'

'The same.'

She reached me and we kissed.

I was pleased to have been leaning with my back against the wall, though I did once wonder whether the lack of mortar would prove its downfall.

We disengaged, and stood gazing into each other, she looking down, possibly a little bashfully, I thought.

'Well, let's walk,' she said. 'Can you lift Benji over the stile?'

I obliged.

'Lucky boy, Benji!' she said as she did so, 'I wish I was you!'

Her happy face was irresistible, and I kissed her, though I thought her comment inane; another misinterpretation would have passed through her mind.

Benji jumped into the adjacent field from the top of the wall, and I clambered over the stile, following him. I turned to assist Hannah, but she didn't take my hand. I didn't mind; in fact, I liked it: she was independent, strong. It was windy, and the strands of hair were lifted from her face.

I became jealous of the wind.

On we walked, to start with in silence. This was a new type

of meeting, and I think we both found it odd. We knew each other, in a way, but were strangers, and in this novel environment I began to wonder what to talk about. This went on for some time as I worried that I even had to think about it. My thoughts were interrupted by her taking my hand. I looked at her and she smiled confidently; maybe she was not having the same doubts as me and was simply enjoying the walk. I wondered how many people thought like that.

The landscape was just fields and grey dry stone walls, with the Levels stretched out below – there was little to comment on, and we both knew we had both been here before.

'It's clear today,' I said. 'You can see for miles. I think the rain last night helped.'

'Yes,' she said, looking at the view.

We walked on.

We reached the kissing gate where Kitty had demanded a kiss, and I let Benji, and then Hannah through.

She did not demand a kiss.

As I passed through the gate, I noticed the ivy again; it hadn't changed, and then, just beyond it, on the top of the well-placed limestone blocks that formed the adjacent wall, I saw a beautiful piece of nature, ancient, extinct, mysterious, but nature nevertheless, and knew this would require investigation.

'Look, some fossil coral.'

'Oh, yes. Isn't it pretty?'

'Yes. It's amazing to think that this grew in a tropical sea and here we find it in a temperate climate under a cold grey sky.

'What do you mean?' she asked.

'It's limestone – part of a coral reef.' I thought it might appear patronising if I explained further, but in any case, I didn't have time to do so; I had found something more exciting and my interest moved on. 'Here's a stone which might break,' I said, picking up a particularly fossiliferous piece of wall, and banging it hard on another rock to split it open.

'Don't do that!' she cried.

I looked round. Many similar stones littered the ground around the wall; one stone missing would make no odds at all, and my supposed vandalism had been worth it: contained within the stone were several beautifully preserved brachiopods.

She peered over.

'It was worth it,' she concluded, to my pleasure.

'Yes. The last time these saw sunlight, the dinosaurs were still a twinkle in God's eye. They must be over three hundred million years old.'

'I can't think about time in those terms.'

Her ignorance annoyed me. I had raised a topic that I thought would be interesting but she did not have much to say. Maybe her religious views precluded her from talking about fossils, being in conflict with the beliefs of a creationist. Maybe she was ignorant about such things, or unwilling to make a reasoned argument.

We walked on, in silence. We evidently viewed things so differently, I had no idea what to say next. But the desire to find out more about her became stronger. It had been so long since I wanted to find out about someone in this way, I did not know where to start. Breaking up the monotony of the fields there came into sight a small, naked, leafless copse of stunted ash waving their boughs in the wind. A question presented itself.

'What's your favourite tree?' I asked.

'Oh, I don't know. How about you?'

'The gingko.'

'The what?'

'The gingko. I like it because it's so ancient. I find it amazing that a single genus can have been around for so long.'

'How long do they live?'

'Some are supposed to have been living when Christ was born. But I didn't mean that. The genus has survived since the Jurassic. Almost two hundred million years.'

Her blank expression told me my words meant little.

'What's a genus?'

'It's a group of organisms which are all related to each other.

Take *Homo sapiens* for example. *Homo* is the genus, *sapiens* the species. *Homo habilis* is an extinct species of bipedal primates much like us, very closely related, except hairier.'

'How do you know he was hairier? Was it preserved?'

'No, far too old, although apart from bones, hair is the last part of your body to decay.'

'Are you telling me all this stuff to provoke me?'

'No, I'm trying to find out about you.'

'You know very well I believe in God.'

'Yes, but why should that preclude us from talking about earth's history?'

'Well, I don't believe in evolution.'

I stopped dead.

'Evolution is not something to believe in. It is a fact. Whether you can reconcile it with your religion is quite another matter.'

'Alex…'

She looked at me, I thought sadly.

'Please…' she started to say. 'Please don't destroy my religion as well as my marriage.'

'Have I destroyed your marriage?'

'Not yet.'

'I don't mean to destroy either.'

Her belief could not have been so strong, I thought, if the mere discussion of evolution would destroy it. Maybe she was scared of knowledge she knew existed, but that she did not know herself, and like so many others, she compartmentalised them in her mind so they all made sense. Made sense to her, at least.

Then she started asking me questions, and the mood lightened.

She wanted to know about me: where I grew up, my family, what interested me (apart from fossils), and I asked her the same, though I already knew her roots. I gradually felt more relaxed, and that progress was being made.

'Why did you leave London?' she asked.

'We didn't want to bring up our children there. We thought there would be less temptation.'

She smiled, though I wondered why.

'Not just that type of temptation. Less greed, less temptation to keep working all hours. Less stress. Look at this view! Not a soul in sight. Not in London!'

'Yes, we are alike,' she concluded, almost wistfully.

And she put her arm round me.

'Not here,' I said. 'It's too hard.'

So she kissed me, making matters worse.

We reached the limestone quarry, of some fame: here had been found the remains of cave-dwelling hominids, together with the bones of rhinoceros and hyena that they had eaten, those animals having been able to inhabit the locality due to the warmer climes that then existed. The bones of the eaten animals showed their tool marks where they had cut the meat from them, and sharpened flints were found in the same stratigraphy. I wondered how good Hannah's local knowledge was, whether she already knew about the quarry and its inhabitants and had chosen to ignore them, or whether she had shunted the remains into the part of her brain separate to her religious beliefs, so conveniently compartmentalising her knowledge, or whether she thought, like fossils, God had placed them there to make the doubtful doubt. Or maybe it had been the Devil that had placed them there, underground, nearer his realm than God's. Would God have allowed such a thing?

'Some of the oldest hominid remains in England were discovered in that quarry.'

'Alex, please…'

'I find it interesting.'

'I feel ignorant. I'm embarrassed.'

Progress!

And enough for now: we talked instead of music, a subject close enough to my heart in any case.

And so we carried on walking, talking, and kissing, safely above the village and prying eyes, but being able to keep our eyes on the whole scene at once. Once we had begun to descend back to the village, we could even see the cathedral in the nearby city, the smallest in England. I knew Kitty wouldn't be far from it, though it did not make me feel uneasy.

The wind blew straight into our faces as we came off the hill. Dark clouds scudded across the sky, and we could see rain falling in vast sheets of grey gradually coming closer. I wondered if we'd be able to get home before it reached us. Once we had descended far enough, the wind subsided as larger trees, not stunted as those on top had been, began to shelter us. When we reached the road, their branches began arching over us, and made a gloomy and dark tunnel beneath. Compared to the vast expanse of sky we had been used to that afternoon, they seemed oppressive, though I was glad of their cover when the rain reached us.

Soon, though, the tree tunnel stopped and the rain became worse. We were nearing the outskirts of the village and the point where we had decided to go our own ways, not least because of the positions of our respective houses. The gorgeous loose strands of Hannah's hair had now stuck to her face, running with rainwater. I still loved them, and tucked them behind her ears so I could see all of her wet beauty at once.

I kissed her, happy in the rain.

Regretfully we parted, and I watched her walk down the lane with Benji, tail again between his legs in disapproval of the soaking he was getting. As they turned a corner, out of view, I began to consider her last words to me, just after she put her hand inside my jacket and ran her gorgeous fingers down my spine, kissing me as she did so.

'I want to come to your house next time.'

At His

As I gazed at the ceiling, things between us seemed somehow quite different.

Perhaps it wasn't so odd he was so different from me. I'd enjoyed our walk. I liked not having to satisfy him. And him me. I think he wanted both.

His conversation, at the time, had bothered me. His knowledge of science was clearly greater than mine, but I'd wondered whether that put blinkers on how he viewed everything else. Not so. When I'd arrived, he'd asked if I wanted a coffee. I'd never made him a coffee at my house. It was always straight to the bedroom. But I'd said yes, to please him. And so I sat in his living room, or library more like. I'd never seen so many books. He'd read them all, apparently. And yes, there were many books on science, history, literature, but also on religion: various histories of Christianity, books on the Gospels, and Christ. And God. Why would an unbeliever read this? I felt deeply insecure in light of his apparent knowledge.

But knowledge was not wisdom, and I knew that my faith had helped me, and that I depended on it, and that I believed. He was scared of faith. Of belief. Even those words scared him, I thought. How can one's mind decide that God is wrong, or does not exist? No, you need that faith to begin to understand. He didn't have it. And on this one point, I felt superior.

And then he kissed my neck, and then my breasts, and his hand, slowly, gently and so so powerfully, felt between my legs, and all thoughts of inferiority and superiority vanished as I realised that in the physical regard, we were equal. We were equal, but, it seemed, above our respective spouses when together in this way. I couldn't stand him not being inside me for a moment longer.

I became embarrassed at how sweaty I had become, but his strong fingers slipped over my collarbone and down my glistening chest with such ease, though he applied his typical passionate pressure, that I didn't care. It became too good to care about anything else…

I flopped down, exhausted.

As did he.

'Christ, I love you,' I said, breathlessly.

He looked at me quizzically.

'What?'

He smiled.

'I love you too. You're quite magnificent.'

I smiled, though I began to realise I was quite flushed, so turned away from him and pulled one of his hands round me, and led it to one of my breasts, which he cradled. I felt wonderful.

That is, until I wondered whether Kitty did the same for him, or more. Sometimes he thought of me, he'd said. Sometimes. How often? How often did she have the legitimate opportunity to do what we'd done.

But I banished these thoughts, squeezing his hand. He squeezed my breast. Such thoughts would only serve mental pain, as did those of sin, against Edward, against my children, against Kitty, against my faith, and against God. I banished those thoughts too, though just before I did so I realised I'd sinned against my father too.

And now I stared at the corner of the pillow, and his bed beneath, their bed, I suppose. No, I mustn't think of that. But I did feel dirtier, sneakier, and more immoral at his house than mine. Was this because we'd started at mine? Was this because it was the first time at his? These questions, and my train of thought were disrupted by his question:

'When did you know?'

'When you walked into the gate.' I heard him smile behind me. 'When did you know?'

'When you stopped smiling at your kids and started smiling at me.'

'In the beginning.'

'In the beginning. But I can only have walked into the gate about a minute later...'

'I never thought I'd believe in love at first sight.'

'I'm not sure I do now,' he said.

I turned to look at him.

'When did you love me, then?' I asked, too obviously hurt.

'In the beginning. But it was a different type of love to the type I feel now.'

I relaxed a little, but didn't understand.

'How has your love changed? Mine has,' I said, partly because it had, and partly to encourage him.

'Can it have been love? Was it just lust? You are very beautiful. But I think it was more than that.' His words came fast. Had he already thought of this? Was his mind working quickly now, and the answers he gave were the ones he'd just thought of, or not yet quite thought of? He continued: 'It must have been more than that. There was some connection...'

'Yes...' I trailed off. It was odd. Edward and I had often talked of our first amorous advances. I suppose most couples do, but this time it was less pure, less perfect. There were huge obstacles in the way. Edward, the children, Kitty. Despite being a hundredfold more powerful than meeting Edward, or indeed any other man, meeting Alex would always be plagued by these difficulties, no matter what happened. Neither of us could change it.

'Did you love me first before or after I walked into the gate?'

'I think before, because I couldn't think of anything else... I'm not sure it matters... I knew something would happen. I knew that if you didn't, I'd ask you.'

I paused.

'Do you think fate brought Benji to you, and you to me?'

'No, luck and co-incidence.'

I chastised myself. I could have written his answer on an envelope before he'd spoken.

Him

She had started it; she had begun to talk about the inception of our relationship. It moved it on too quickly. It reminded me of Kitty doing the same, but I hadn't minded it then; there was no third party, no problems: it had just been her and me. Now, I knew she was married to Edward, and I to Kitty. We both slept with our spouses. The thought disturbed me. How could she, after having kissed me so passionately, she, after inviting me into her house, her life, her... How could she lie there talking about how we met?

I didn't want to think, yet, now, how things would happen henceforth, but I knew, even if Edward became ancient history, his name would make my stomach turn. How long for, I wondered? I knew not, but he was, after all, the father of her children. I had not had this problem before. I had once met a boyfriend of Kitty's, though she never talked of him to me since our relationship had developed into that of more than friends. Kitty would never have done that.

Her

His face had changed. Though his arms were around me, and mine around him, his whole countenance had changed.

'What's the matter?'

'Nothing.'

'Tell me. I already know you better than that.'

'Damn you!' he said, smiling. But his smile would not put me off.

'Tell me, Alex?'

'Just daft thoughts.'

I opened my mouth to push him further and he sighed. Maybe some things were better left unsaid, so I stopped. But I wanted to know.

'I won't mind, whatever it is.'

'Our meeting can never be perfect,' he said, a little crossly.

'I'm sorry, darling.'

An Invitation

Once Hannah had gone, her talking of how we met became the more bitter the more I thought of it. Before marrying Kitty, I had promised myself never to ignore my emotions. But now, for the first time in years, I shut them out. Then I realised that since meeting Hannah I had already been keeping thoughts from my wife for the first time since I'd asked her to marry me. But, I reflected, this was not as unhealthy as keeping thoughts from myself, as well I knew from past unhappy imaginings that Kitty had helped me stamp out. It was necessary, though.

I was glad when Kitty returned home; we had a pleasant evening together. She made me feel things were vaguely normal again. Hannah coming to my house had me feel a little uneasy; it been invasive, but I had at the time supposed it fair. It would be my turn to invent excuses should things not be totally normal in Kitty's eyes, but though I was not too worried about it then, when we went upstairs to bed, I found it profoundly odd that I had last been there with Hannah. I was pleased when Kitty said she wanted to go straight to sleep. We both did just that, and in the morning I mused that I had slept better than I had done since meeting Hannah.

The next morning Kitty announced that it was my birthday the week after – not because she thought I'd forgotten – but by way of introducing the topic. She had taken the liberty, she said, of inviting my best friend and best man, Danny, her sister, Rosie, and our mutual friends James and Emily, through whom we had originally met. Danny was only allowed to come if he did not try it on with Rosie, and I agreed to brief him accordingly. These were friends from our old life, from London, and I was pleased that they were coming; their presence, even in our little house in the village, would, for the weekend at least, make me forget Hannah.

Then Kitty said how lovely it would be to invite some of our new friends: the vicar, Dr and Mrs Parsons and Hannah and Edward.

'They are hardly our friends,' I began, but she silenced me by proclaiming me antisocial.

'I'm not that old. I begin to feel middle aged by having to invite the vicar and local GP!' I protested.

Eventually she conceded that the Parsons might be a little old, and the vicar certainly too religious; the thought of saying grace before we could tuck in clinched it, and they were removed from the planned proceedings.

I thought I had got away with it, but she said I ought I go round and ask Hannah and Edward before they made other plans. She pointed out that we owed them an invite after their Christmas party; there was little I could do to protest, and I did not want to protest too much.

Her

I'd left his house uncertain and unhappy. He'd undoubtedly been cold with me. It had never happened before. Why? Our meeting had been imperfect, he'd said. Of course it had. I had never thought of another man until he came along. I'd known Edward for years. Didn't he understand that? Couldn't he see how important that made him? I became angry at his narrow-mindedness. Did he just want me to divorce Edward and be done with it? To never mention him again? The father of my children? I took my anger out on Edward, unfairly. Guilt again racked me, and I even dreamed of my father, telling me how evil I'd been. In my nightmare, he'd even used the word *slut*. I wasn't one of them. I loved Edward but was in love with Alex. I loved Alex but was in love with Edward. Which way round was it?

Did it matter?

Was I evil?

These ruminations bounced round my head for days.

We had just finished washing up, and I'd been crashing the pots and pans as the latest incarnation of this argument tormented me, even though the children were in bed and could probably hear.

Edward had kindly asked me what the matter was.

'Nothing,' I had said, before throwing the dishcloth in the sink and departing for some solitude in the living room.

But Edward followed me to the sofa.

'I'm just going to draw the curtains,' I said, as an excuse not to be drawn too close to him, and jumped up to do so.

My hands had just reached up to grab the curtains when, in the light shining out from the room, I saw Alex fumbling with the latch of our garden gate.

I drew the curtains in a flash.

I fancied I saw his head look up as his guiding light became dark, but I did not catch his eye. I hoped it had seemed like a light going out to him, but why should I care? What the fuck was he doing here? His games were getting beyond a joke. His jokes weren't amusing. I was fuming. How dare he invade my life when not asked?

Him

She opened the door before I could knock.

'What in God's name are you doing here?' she hissed. Didn't she know that hisses travelled further than low speech?

'I've come to invite you and Edward to my birthday party.'

She looked at me incredulously.

'Kitty's idea. We owe you an invite. You're the only people in the village we know our age.'

'Well, I hope we're busy! When?'

'Saturday week.'

'Damn. We're free! Well. It'll depend on a babysitter.'

I heard Edward grunt as he evidently levered himself up from whatever he'd been sitting on, and his heavy footsteps approached. Thankfully, in some respects only, a cheery hello and short chat followed. I tried hard to be friendly, to smile at this man, insanely jealous that he had married Hannah, and could sleep with her every night, and sometimes – how often? – do more. But I pitied him too, perhaps in a cruel, derogatory way.

To my dismay, and Hannah's, he gaily volunteered to telephone the babysitter then and there to give me a definite answer without me having to wait.

The babysitter could do it.

It was settled.

It was odd not being able to kiss Hannah goodbye, and when Edward put his arm round her as they stood waiting for me to successfully navigate my way through their garden gate, I felt sick.

A Birthday

Her

I suppose deep down I knew our lives would become further entwined, but the thought of bringing our spouses into the equation had remained locked in a place that I hardly dared open. Now Alex had opened the door of that place for me, and this new problem joined the others going round my head.

When he'd invited us, his face had told me that he hadn't wanted to as much I didn't want to go. It was funny that our spouses had effectively orchestrated the acceptance of Alex's invitation, though they hadn't spoken to each other. If it had been left to us, the guilty parties, we would have invented excuses. I might not even have had to have told Edward, though I soon left this thought behind: what if Kitty should meet Edward in the village and spoke of it? Now, no loose ends must be left, however trivial. Everything needed to be thought through. I felt like a spy, or codebreaker at Bletchley Park, sworn to secrecy for years about something huge I couldn't tell anyone, though I already had. Then I felt belittled for making such a comparison. I wasn't winning a war.

But I began to feel less guilty about the affair. Maybe guilt had saturated my thoughts, my being, my soul, and now these rotten parts of me were used to it.

Maybe that was so, but there was a new type of guilt that could still penetrate and worm its way into my thoughts. It was a guilt that originated not from Edward, or my father, or God.

It originated from Alex.

This unwanted but almost exciting guilt crept into my thoughts when I realised that I was enjoying this new life of mine.

I felt guilty to be excited about Alex.

And conflicting feelings of intrigue and dread also came over me, though they originated from the same source: Kitty. I was intrigued to see he how was with her. How he spoke. How he smiled. How they interacted. But these thoughts also filled me a simultaneous dread. I didn't want to witness these things, though I longed to know the answers. But I knew that as soon as I had them, I would want to dispose of them. And such things are hard to forget.

I wondered if he thought I was still angry with him because of his coming over to invite us. I was sorry for it. I should have realised he'd come for a purpose, but it had become difficult to think rationally or logically about anything to do with Alex. But I couldn't ask him or apologise. I didn't see him again until his birthday.

Him

My birthday came quickly, and with it, Rosie, Danny, James and Emily.

In the morning, Kitty had collected Rosie from the little station where a few direct trains from London stopped each day. Pretty Rosie whose luck with men meant that she always seemed to be single in spite of her beauty. Many would argue she was the prettier sister, and although they were pretty in very different ways – you would never guess they were sisters – they had both inherited good genes. I was surprised she had come; enticing Rosie with an invitation to anywhere more than two miles from Trafalgar Square was like trying to prise a limpet off a rock with one's bare hands. The two sisters gossiped and giggled as they were inclined to do after a few weeks of absence, and it pleased me to see them, Kitty especially, so happy. Rosie's arrival had already begun to make things seem as they had in the past, and I hoped that once the others came, the party would not be the ordeal I had feared it might be.

After lunch, James and Emily arrived, gay as ever, and by

teatime, Danny bowled up, earlier than expected, but still two hours late. It was great fun to have them all there, and we caught up on news, and talked of old times in London, which now, though only a few months ago, seemed as if they had never existed but in my memory. They were all doing the same things, drinking at the same haunts, seeing the same friends, except of course Danny, who had being seeing a new girl each month, only to discover she was not quite all she was cracked up to be, or perhaps she finding out he was not either; I never knew which way round it was, though of course he never admitted the latter. I was happy they all still enjoyed that life, but happier to hear their stories and to live the city life vicariously through them. I knew Kitty thought the same from the little looks she gave me, and through a squeeze of my hand when she had told them how happy we were to have moved to the country.

They asked us of village life, and I felt rather uncomfortable when neither of us could really say that much about it. There was no tube, less money, much less stress, but more mud and many more smells of cow shit. We could tell them little about our new friends, since we had few; after moving, the house needed redecorating, our things unpacking, new furniture to fill the void which was three times as big as our old flat, and country life to settle into; we had only just made things ship-shape. I don't think they really understood.

Rosie wanted to know if there were any eligible bachelors.

'The vicar is pretty dishy,' I said, laughing.

Kitty told me off, and Rosie asked how old he was.

'Oh, pretty young. I'd say he has a few years before he starts drawing his pension!'

Danny wanted to know if there were any eligible farmers' daughters.

'None that I've met. Have you got any business cards with your photo on that I could distribute if I chance on any?'

Not even Danny had thought of this.

We all laughed a great deal at James' anecdotes, Emily looking on in feigned disapproval, but entirely failing to conceal her love for him. In such moments, I was envious of them, of their simple, loving relationship, unaffected by others. But I was pleased Kitty had invited them: it was the best birthday present I could have wished for.

And before we knew it, the doorbell rang.

Such was the company, I had almost totally forgotten that Hannah and Edward were due to arrive, though the nagging feeling in the recesses of my mind became clear when they did.

Kitty answered the door and they came in to where we all sat.

Everyone rose to greet the new guests.

'Rosie!' exclaimed Hannah.

'You know each other?' I asked, stupidly, stupefied.

'For years!' said Hannah, feigning a smile.

If I could tell she was forcing her mouth into that awkward shape, so could Edward.

Could Rosie?

'The funny thing is,' said Hannah, 'I wrote you a postcard yesterday, and posted it on the way here!'

Edward looked sharply at her.

Rosie thought this a wonderful coincidence, and said she had wondered whether it was the same village we had moved to, and whether we had met.

'Well, it is the same village, but we've only met a couple of times. In church, and at our Christmas drinks party,' said Hannah. 'It really is very kind of you to have us,' she added, to Kitty. 'It feels much more of a special occasion than the drinks party.'

Then Edward asked if Hannah was all right.

And indeed, I became worried that she was not: all the colour had left her face.

'Oh, I've been feeling pretty rotten all day. It must have been the walk. I'll be fine.'

Edward said that if had known, he wouldn't have allowed her out of the house.

'That's why I didn't tell you, darling!' Hannah tried to joke.

Her

How easy it would have been to avoid the whole thing. This new disaster. One little lie would have prevented us from going, and the doting Edward would have looked after his ill wife with his usual devotion, not realising the only illness she suffered from was love, and the terror that loving someone other than your husband brings. But lying hadn't even crossed my mind.

Him

'Who'd like a drink?' I asked, mainly because I did, but also to manoeuvre us out of this awkward scene.

It worked.

Orders were taken, and further introductions and chatter between Kitty and our guests ensued, although it was true that the conversation seemed to centre on how extraordinary it was that Hannah and Rosie should know each other, and what a small world it was.

Too bloody small.

It turned out that they had worked together when Hannah had first moved to London, and although they saw little of each other since Hannah had moved out, they still had their six-monthly chats on the phone and the odd coffee when Hannah went up to Town.

'But we haven't seen each other for getting on for a year,' said Hannah. 'Gosh, I must come to London soon!' she said, to Rosie's enthusiastic agreement.

The idea struck me as disastrous. I imagined them gossiping as Rosie had done that morning with her sister, and the idea filled me with horror, though I hoped Hannah would not be daft enough to utter one breath about the happenings in our sleepy little village since Christmas.

The dynamic changed when Hannah and Edward arrived, but not in a bad way. Once we had settled into our seats, Kitty and Hannah next to each other on one of the sofas, the chatter began again. Anecdotes between my old friends became less frequent, though more carefully chosen and therefore funnier: but the conversation shifted to allow our old friends and new guests, and indeed us, to get to know more about each other. Where Hannah was concerned, I suddenly realised that I had to unlearn everything I knew about her, in order not to raise suspicion from Kitty or Edward. It was surprisingly hard to do so, and I let the others do most of the questioning, listening with interest to the answers. Whenever Edward spoke, I tried to shut out his words: I did not want to learn more about him, or listen to him speak. Despite this, the more I did learn, the more I began to wonder if there was anything *to* know. His rather flat voice began to make me angry. How had this magnificent, fun, beautiful woman married such a non-entity of a man?

Then I overheard Hannah say to Kitty, 'I must pop to the loo.'

And Hannah waited for Kitty's directions, though the last time she had been there she had been totally naked.

It was a nice touch; she was becoming better at our game.

Hannah returned to a slight lull in the conversation, and made use of it by asking: 'The paintings in the hall must be Kitty's?' We had not talked about them when she'd been here illicitly; there were many things to talk about and we couldn't cover everything.

Kitty put her straight, and she blushed.

'I would never have guessed!' she said. 'They're wonderful, they really are! What other surprises are you hiding, Alex?' she asked, foolishly.

I tried to laugh off her compliment, and her question, but was pleased she had said it and asked it: her blush had been real, and everyone had noticed it.

And then Kitty announced that we should eat, so we did.

Danny had engineered a seat next to Rosie, and was particularly attentive to her, offering her everything he could, and ensuring her comfort, though she became less at ease because of it. I noticed her smile at her sister, and I think they were thinking the same thing. Edward sat next to his wife, who had to ask him to pass her various victuals, though his plate was already full.

We must have all been hungry because Kitty's food – she was a splendid cook – began to disappear rapidly amongst more chatter between us. And although I enjoyed hearing our friends enjoy themselves, I only became engrossed in the conversation when Hannah spoke. It was odd that she should hold my attention so much more than my established friends. It was odd listening to her telling everyone things about her that I did not even know. It was to be expected: our total conversation time could not have been that great, but I became jealous that she had not told me these things first. I didn't like finding out about her in this rather second-hand kind of way.

After we had eaten – which in the end took some time because of the chatter and number of courses – and had coffee, it was getting late, and Kitty gave me the nod to clear the table. Danny was engrossed in conversation with Rosie, and although it seemed a shame to stop him in mid-flow, I knew I would be doing him a favour.

'Danny!' I said, rising with a pile of pudding bowls from my end of the table.

To his credit, he began collecting dirty crockery immediately, Rosie's first, of course, and followed me through to the kitchen. As soon as we were alone, Danny expressed his interest in Rosie and asked what he thought his chances were.

'Pretty low, I'm afraid. Kitty has already told her all about you.'

'That buggers things!'

'Yes, I should say it does,' I said grinning, and he smiled back. I was pleased to see that Danny hadn't changed, accepting with good humour that this rosy fish may have already slipped through his Rosie shaped net.

Then he said he thought Hannah was pretty gorgeous.

The idea filled me with horror.

Danny was a good-looking man; furthermore, despite being religious, his morals were such that marriage would not put him off in the least. Hannah might be getting a taste for someone other than her rather vapid husband, and she might go for a man

71

who was outwardly holy. I recognised my thoughts were panic-stricken and stupid: Hannah would not be interested in him if she loved me, and Danny would never seriously entertain the idea of leaving London for only one woman. But perhaps even before I had thought this, I had said:

'Don't even think about it, Danny.'

I never called him Danny in that tone; he was one of those people whose name I never added to the end of sentences. For a split second, I wondered if he would notice, but his response soon put pay to that.

He had asked if I fancied a piece of her.

'She's married, for God's sake!' I whispered, desperately trying to recover myself, though I knew I would never normally have said such a thing – to Danny, at least.

He recognised this, and told me so.

'Village life is not the same as London. It's different here.'

He thought things could be much dirtier in a village.

He insight shocked me.

'Yes, Danny, I'm sure you're right, but the point is, they are new friends, and I don't want to upset the apple cart.'

This seemed to satisfy him, and he remarked that it would be better not to waste good cider apples.

In earlier days, I would have told Danny my darkest, most immoral secrets and furtive thoughts, and I expect he thought I would now as well; there was, after all, no reason why not. But there was no way I would tell him about Hannah. She was too special. There was too much to lose. I was married now, no longer a bachelor in London.

Just then Rosie came in, carrying a tray of empty coffee cups. Danny, perhaps embarrassed in the face of Rosie, took his leave and returned to the party.

Rosie asked if we knew many other people in the village.

'No, not really. We've hardly had a chance to socialise, there has been so much to do.'

Edward's arrival in the kitchen and subsequent announcement

that Hannah and he must depart to relieve the babysitter thankfully stopped any further questioning from her.

We joined the others and farewells were said, Hannah agreeing to tell Rosie when she was next coming to London, and Edward saying that we must come over for dinner. They departed to my relief: tiredness can make the guilty forget, and those who lie must have good memories. But it seemed to me that they had departed without either of us giving anything away, and I was pleased.

The rest of us chatted a little longer, then we all went to bed.

'Thank you for a lovely birthday party,' I said to Kitty as we lay in bed. 'It was good fun. I'm glad Hannah and Edward came.'

And I was, in a way.

She had been glad too, and was pleased I had enjoyed it.

'I hope Danny is behaving himself,' I said. Even in the country we did not have enough rooms for each of our guests, so he was sleeping in the same room as Rosie. 'But I expect Rosie knows how to handle herself!'

Kitty sleepily mumbled her agreement and I thought of Rosie.

It was extraordinary that she and Hannah should have worked together, and I was thankful that they hadn't seen each other since before our arrival to the village.

James and Emily had helped hold things together that evening, I mused. It was lovely to see them so obviously in love, but more importantly, I was very pleased that at many of the critical moments in conversation, one of them had asked an innocent question, unwittingly leading things away from the only truth that needed to remain hidden. I thanked God they had come, only realising that I had afterwards, but not feeling stupid for having done so.

Then it struck me as odd that after coffee, in the kitchen, Rosie had asked me if we knew anyone else in the village. Her question had been almost prying, almost confrontational, and the subject had been brought up once already. Had she been there on the first occasion?

Afterwards

Him

The next morning, nothing remarkable happened. At breakfast, Rosie, who came down first, complained of Danny's snoring.

'He's never told me he snored,' I said.

Rosie said a man would be unlikely to tell anyone he snored, assuming he knew he snored himself.

We spent the morning chatting, had a magnificent Sunday lunch and a walk to walk it off, thankfully avoiding Henry Lane and the hills beyond. Afterwards, our guests began to talk about leaving. I think they had all enjoyed their sojourn to the country, but were equally looking forward to returning to more familiar surroundings. Rosie said she was looking forward to reading her postcard – what news, she wondered, did it contain? During a conversation about returning to the city, she said that London seemed far less complicated than village life.

They all departed, James and Emily giving Rosie a lift, Danny driving off in his sports car, alone, but all back to London, back to their own lives.

Her

When I'd got home, I hadn't been able to sleep. The evening hadn't been a total disaster. Neither Alex nor I had made any obvious mistakes, but Rosie! Rosie! How could I have known?

My postcard idea had been a good one, and at the time, I'd thought it inspired. I did, from time to time, send her the odd postcard, so it I hoped it wouldn't be too suspicious. But what would I write? As I lay there, tossing and turning, ten variants of the same words went round my head.

In church the next day, I kept looking round to see if Alex and Kitty, and indeed Rosie and the others were coming. Even once the service had started, I was so fidgety – more so than the children – that Edward asked what was wrong.

'Nothing, darling,' I whispered, though my face could not have told the same story. An excuse could be invented if needs be, but not now. Not in church. Besides, I was so worried, that I didn't care about what Edward thought just then.

After lunch, I settled down to write the postcard, though just as the right words finally began to formulate themselves, Edward interrupted me by asking what I was doing.

'Just writing Alex and Kitty and thank-you note,' I said. 'Do you want to put anything?'

He thought I'd do a good enough job on my own.

So after writing a thank-you note to Alex and Kitty, I started:

Little Cottage, Friday a.m.

Dear Rosie,

Great to catch up on the phone the other day. I'm sorry things didn't work out with Tom, but it sounds as if you're better off without him. Things have moved on since we last spoke. He's left the village. Things weren't working out for them here. I don't think it was to do with me. I think they both missed the city life. Last time I saw him, he said so. He had a job offer he couldn't refuse. So I am left bereft, but happy. Things started so wonderfully, but even now I realise it was just lust – nothing more. I love Edward, and I hope my sins can be forgiven. How I wish things were as they were six months ago! Anyway, we're off to dinner with some new friends tomorrow, so hopefully I won't be as lonely now. I must come to London soon, and when I do, you'll be the first person I call! See you soon I hope!

Love,

Hannah xxx

I had written all the way across the postcard on purpose – I had to write fairly small in any case – and put it in an envelope, sealing it. It pained me to write such things. There now existed written evidence of an affair – a different affair, invented to cover the real one – but an affair nevertheless. There was no alternative, though, and I had to hope Rosie would be its only reader. I would post it in town in the morning, and popped it into my handbag so I wouldn't forget. The postmark would read Monday – if the date was legible – but there was no Sunday collection in the village anyway. She would be none the wiser. The coincidence of seeing her was far greater than that of me having posted her a note, and I hoped she'd take Alex's way of looking at such things. It was all I could do.

That night, instead of fretting about what to write on the postcard, I worried that Rosie had already told Kitty about my infidelity, and that even as I lay here, it was all over. But, I reasoned, if Rosie had been so suspicious, it would have been over at the party. Besides, Rosie was a measured, sensible girl and not one for jumping to conclusions or destroying her sister's marriage over something she knew very little of. Despite these vaguely comforting thoughts, I didn't sleep a wink.

I knew I must speak to Alex about it. If he knew, he would be armed with the knowledge to be able to defend himself should the need arise. I needed to see him soon. And so, the next morning, after taking Lucy to school and Harry to playschool, I posted the enveloped postcard and headed back to see Alex, thank you note at the ready, should an excuse be required.

It was not.

He was alone; he told me so without a word.

'Good to see you again so soon!' was all he said before he closed the door behind me. I tore his shirt off, and it stayed on the hall floor as we progressed bedwards.

'That was a close shave,' he said afterwards.

'Yes.'

'With Rosie.'

'Yes. Closer than you might think.'

He leaned up on one elbow, his chest muscles moving

magnificently as he did so. I had to touch them.

'Meaning what?'

'I don't see her often, but we chat on the phone.'

'You didn't?'

His question didn't need answering.

'Don't worry, I've never mentioned your name.'

'I can't believe you're so bloody stupid.'

He jumped out of bed, and began pacing the room, a mixture of anger and concentration across his face.

'So she knows you're carrying on with another man?'

'From London.'

God! He looked handsome when he was cross! I told him about the relevance of the postcard comment, and the contents of the postcard, word for word. I'd spent so long thinking about what to write, I could remember it exactly. This calmed him down significantly, though he was still out of bed, arms crossed, thinking hard. It was hard to take him seriously, naked.

'Well, I suppose the postcard will patch things up nicely, assuming she buys it,' he concluded, which did make me feel better too.

'She's no reason not to buy it.'

'Unless she's very suspicious. Is that why you went white? It looked like you'd seen a ghost.'

'I had, I suppose.'

'Well, you wriggled your way out of that one rather well too.'

'Thank you,' I said smiling.

He glanced up from the spot on the floor he'd previously been staring at, and held my gaze for some while, his eyes finding mine, but his thoughts elsewhere. I didn't interrupt, and eventually looked away, such was the intensity of his stare.

'Is this all a game to you?' he said, jumping on the bed, and burying me in bedclothes.

I was forgiven.

But he stopped as soon as he'd started.

'What?' I mumbled, through a pillow.

'Is there anything else you haven't told me?'

I freed myself.

'No.'

'Good.'

'Have you told anyone else?'

'Yes.'

'For God's sake!'

I'd made him angry again. The first time had been bearable. Even endearing, in a way, but I could see he was worried, and I could see why.

'I'm sorry, darling.'

'Don't call me that.'

I didn't know what to say.

'Why?' I said eventually.

'I can't bear it when you say it to Edward.'

'Sorry.'

I was, but I had to make it better.

'Don't worry about her. She's my sister.'

'I didn't even knew you had a sister.'

'You never asked.'

And with that, I think he must have seen how upset I was. He sat on the edge of the bed, his penis looking small and impotent for the first time, and we hugged. Not a terribly comfortable hug due to him sitting and me lying, but it became quite wonderful when he slipped under the covers, and I felt the entire length of his body close up to mine. Within seconds, I felt his impotency vanish with his anger, and my sadness with it.

Again, I felt at one with him, like I never had with Edward.

It never lasted long enough, though in some ways, too long.

'I love you,' I said, between breaths.

'I love you too.'

I wrapped my arms round him, and stuck a leg between his, both of us lying there for some time in happy silence.

'Was it terribly awkward having Edward in your house?'

'Not as bad as I'd thought it might be. It helps that he's a reserved sort of man.'

'Kind though.'

'I daresay.'

'On the night of our drinks party, I said to Lucy and Harry, "Goodnight and sleep tight. Mind the bugs don't bite." All I could think about was whether you were downstairs. That felt odd. You're not their father.'

'I was downstairs though.'

'I knew *I* wouldn't sleep tight that night.'

'I didn't either.'

And then he went silent, and I couldn't think of anything else to say.

Him

She had again started talking about when we had met, and it sickened me that she could still talk about it, given that Edward was still very much in evidence, and that he had so recently been in my house.

But she obviously liked thinking and talking about it, and I forgave her; it was hard not to, her lying next to me. I tried not to think about it when she departed – things were different when she was not there, and my imagination was less easily controlled in her absence. Thinking had become dangerous.

It was a week later, at Little Cottage, when I saw her again. In that time, despite my best endeavours to the contrary, a question I had begun to ask myself became ever more prominent in my thoughts, and I knew I must talk her about it. But after I had arrived, Hannah was not herself: I could tell something was on her mind, and I decided to let her voice her apparent worries first.

Childish Questions

Her

I suppose Alex had sowed the initial seeds of doubt. If it had been anyone else, those seeds would have fallen on rocky ground, the roots withering away in the heat of my faith. But Alex had provided some nourishment for the roots to take hold.

And now, to my surprise, Lucy – who, like Harry, I had separated from Alex to protect both these my children, and myself – had begun to be curious, and was adding her own little, childish, ignorant, but very pertinent questions to the turmoil of my thoughts. I didn't know whether to discuss it with Alex for some days after Lucy had begun to question me, but as I lay in his arms, in my bed, I knew I must.

But I wasn't quite ready.

The right moment in conversation would need to be created.

'Any more news of Rosie?'

'No,' he said. 'You?'

'No.'

'Good.'

'Yes.'

There was little else to say, and he didn't say anything further.

'Alex?'

'Yes?'

'I want to talk to you about Lucy.'

'Oh yes?' he said, not stirring.

'She's been asking questions.'

'What questions?' he said a little faster than usual, a small amount of worry evident in his tone.

'Difficult ones to answer.'

'Well, you seem to be astute, and good at answering difficult questions to adults!' he said, amused.

'The answers themselves are easy, Alex. It's the afterthoughts that are left behind that are trickier.'

'I don't follow...'

'Sorry. I'm not coming at this from the simplest of angles.'

'No.'

'I was reading the Bible with Lucy the other night –'

'Ah! Catch them young!' he said.

I had expected it, and I wasn't surprised, nor, to my surprise, was I angry. But I didn't agree. I didn't disagree.

'Lucy asked, "What is our trespasses?"'

He smiled at her question.

'"Our sins," I told her, "Bad things we know we shouldn't do." She asked if we would go to Hell if we do trespasses. I said, yes, if we don't say we're sorry.'

'You don't seriously believe –'

'Let me finish.'

'Sorry.'

'Then she asked if, when we are naughty, but say sorry, whether it would be all right. I said it would be, but that we should try not to be naughty in the first place. She looked so fearful at the thought of going to Hell. She asked if I was ever naughty. I said that everyone is naughty sometimes, for unkind things we do, or unkind thoughts, but as long as we tried to do what we thought was the right thing, and said sorry when we knew we were wrong, God would forgive us. Then she looked pleased that there were ways of avoiding Hell. Or maybe she was pleased I had admitted that I wasn't perfect either.'

I had finished.

Silence.

'Well, I'm not sure what you want me say,' said Alex in the end.

'Whatever springs to mind. I think I know your views well enough by now. I wouldn't have brought it up otherwise.'

There was a pause, but I could see he was thinking.

Eventually he spoke.

'I think it is good, in a way, that you teach your children the Christian stories. Christian morality is a good way of leading one's life.' He paused for a wry smile. 'But to teach them that they'll go to Hell if they are bad seems ridiculous. I don't know how anyone can believe in either Heaven or Hell. Heaven arises from the human condition of hope: the idea gives hope to the hopeless, and has done through the centuries. Tell the huddled masses that there is some point, that there is something *else*, something to believe in, and something to look forward to, and of course they'll want to believe. Likewise, Hell is designed to make unbelievers too fearful not to believe. Both have made the Church richer and more powerful, mainly to feed the vanity, stomachs and greed of those in charge. To teach seven-year-olds about either is unfair. They have neither the knowledge nor wisdom to make an informed decision themselves.'

'How can you say that Heaven and Hell are *designed*? Jesus himself spoke of both.'

'Did he? Did he talk *explicitly* of Hell? Yes, he talked of it and its fires extensively in the Bible, but he mentions Hades as a place of torment only once, in Luke. But that was written long after his death, about 80 or 90 AD, sixty years after his death. That would be like writing about the Second World War now, but with no books, no films, no photos. Just word of mouth. Imagine the stories that would have come from that, being passed from soldiers to their friends, sons, grandsons, each time their memories elaborating the stories a tiny bit to make them more impressive or exciting to the recipient. How many times in your own life have you told someone something that you have experienced *exactly* as it happens? Danny is a great proponent of never letting the truth get in the way of a good story, and it's partly why he's so entertaining. I don't think any the worse of him because of it: he doesn't even *mean* to do it sometimes. And that's why it becomes so dangerous in historical terms. And compare the Bible stories to our own, more recent history which is still in living memory. In a way, it is an unfair comparison *because* technology and communications have been so much better in our recent past, but imagine Hitler in biblical times. Jesus touched thousands of people in just a few years of preaching; Hitler reached millions. If he'd have claimed a divine link, more easily done back then, imagine the consequences... I've never thought of it like myself before, but it's an interesting thought.'

'I don't see how you can compare them. It's a daft idea.'

'Yes, it is a little. But back to Jesus and Hell. The gospels hardly mention Hell, and when they do, it's only in passing...'

'The gospels are the word of God.'

'What do you mean by that?'

I couldn't answer.

'I don't think you know what you mean,' he continued, 'It is something that is said so often in Church, people believe it because of its familiarity, because everyone says it. No-one stops to think.'

I was silent. My head was awash with new knowledge and thoughts, and they were scaring me. I *had* never stopped to think in this way. It intrigued me, and terrified me. I hadn't wanted my marriage unsteadied, but in a kind of perverse way, I loved it, and now Alex was attacking my faith. I had thought that even if he could touch my heart, he couldn't touch my soul, but now he was beginning to, and I was beginning to love that, too. He was smiling. The Devil was smiling too. His avatar was powerful, and I loved him.

'Look, I'm sorry,' he said. Putting a hand on my shoulder. 'I know our views differ,' he said more quietly after his enthusiastic outburst previously. I appreciated his concern, but deep down, I wanted this. I had, after all, brought up the subject.

'You did bring it up. You must have known what I was going to say!' he said, smiling.

I nodded, smiling, and he seemed to relax again.

'It is interesting,' I admitted. He now knew I wasn't cross, and this was enough to make him start up again.

'Have you ever asked yourself about Hell?' he asked.

He didn't wait for an answer.

'The simplest questions pose big problems for the Christian faith. Why would an all-loving God allow his sheep to roast in eternity? Why does an all-powerful God allow the Devil to exist? Why should we be tempted? What purpose does this serve God, who must have a sadistic streak in him to allow it? Jesus said, "You must come to God through me." What of the countless millions who lived before Jesus, or have lived since and never heard of him? What of the Jews? What of the Buddhists, Muslims, Sikhs and members of other world faiths, all morally sound and ancient? Will they all be condemned downstairs for leading good lives simply because their faiths do not contain Jesus as the central figure? You see… simple questions… impossible answers.'

They were, and I was sure books could and have been written on each, and then I wondered whether he'd read them. There was too much to think about all at once just then, but I did resolve to consider some of the points he raised when I had a little more time to think, when I could rationalise them without Alex challenging my thoughts as soon as I'd had them.

I sighed.

He took my sigh as a sign of weakness and I saw that he was about to use to his advantage in another verbal attack. I did not have the arguments, and therefore the confidence to counter it before it began.

'But let's put aside these theological arguments,' he began. 'You already know that I have respect for Christian ethics and morals: it is impossible to criticise many of them. But some cannot be taken too seriously or literally.'

I opened my mouth to silence him. Even I knew that he was taking a step too far. To my surprise, he paused, to allow me to speak, but his face, confident in what he was about to say, silenced me.

'You,' he continued, 'do not even abide by the most basic Jewish and Christian ethics.'

He paused to allow me to dispute his claim, but I had no idea where his argument was leading.

'The Ten Commandments,' he said. 'Thou shalt not commit adultery. Thou shalt not covet thy neighbour's wife. How can you believe that, when what we have so feels so natural, so right? Who is Moses, or God to say that what we are doing is wrong? Do you think it is wrong?'

'It is wrong in one sense,' I said. 'But it feels so right.'

He nodded.

He was right, after all. Our love was the most natural thing in the world.

'Sorry,' he said. 'Enough?'

I nodded.

I had another question I wanted to pose, though it frightened me almost more than the prospect of losing my faith. I had no idea if he'd been wondering about it, whether the issue was burning in his mind, as it was mine; or whether he cared, or whether he, like me, was almost too frightened to ask. But to ask it was inevitable – it couldn't not be asked, at some stage. In some ways, asking it earlier would be better, though it might destroy what we had instantly.

Now the moment when I'd decided to ask him had come, I couldn't quite do it. Instead, I leaned over, and kissed him, still desperately in love with him, his lips, his body, despite our minds being so different. He accepted my advance, as he always did, and we didn't speak for another half an hour.

'What do you want to ask me?' he said as we lay together. Did he know me this well already? Edward would never have said that. Despite our cognitive and rational thoughts being so wildly different, Alex was so attuned to my emotions, my needs, it scared me, as with so many things with him. But as it scared me, it excited me. Were my emotions never to be stable with him?

'You're thinking that Edward would have never known to ask, aren't you?' he said, at once scaring me more, and sending lightning down my spine and limbs.

'Yes…'

'It was your expression of disbelief…'

'Oh.'

I rolled towards him and buried my face in his chest.

'Well,' he said, my face still hidden, 'are you going to ask me?'

I knew I must and without hesitation I withdrew my face from his chest, looked at him, and quite simply said it.

'What is going to happen between us?'

Doubt

Him

In bed that night, Kitty announced that she was going to London to see Rosie. She said that seeing her at my birthday had reminded her how much she missed her, and, she said, a dose of London life with her socialite sister would do her a world of good.

'Why do you need a dose of London life? Do you miss it?' I asked.

She did miss it, but sweetly said she was enjoying village life, and that I must not worry because she did not hanker for the life we had left behind. It did comfort me. I needed reassurance. Guilt plays with the mind in ways that are not always obvious.

I was pleased: Hannah had said that Edward would be away that same weekend, and I might be able to spend an entire night with her, a previously unthought-of pleasure. Could she rid herself of her children to allow us such precious time together?

It was only after this initial thought had passed that I wondered what Rosie might say to Kitty. Rosie, who had received a postcard from Hannah explicitly outlining an adulterous affair with an unknown man from London. That man had moved out of the village, though, closing one danger but immediately opening another: *because* the affair had finished, would Rosie think it less important to keep it a secret? Had Hannah asked her to keep it a secret? How close were they? Were Rosie and Hannah close enough as friends to stop Rosie sharing such personal information with her own sister? Would Rosie believe the contents of the postcard, or would she see through the deliberate deceitfulness? Would Hannah's reaction at seeing Rosie at my birthday party have inflamed Rosie's suspicion? Was Rosie observant enough to guess? Had Danny said anything to Rosie about my reaction to his question about Hannah? Would this add to Rosie's suspicion? My mind whirred through these questions, and more, fleetingly, acknowledging them to be paranoid musings, but not dismissing the possibility of any of them happening. I became almost panic-stricken. And underneath the panic, the rising fear – at first hiding beneath my furious questioning – began now to articulate itself with a clarity that made me wonder why I had not recognised it before; I acknowledged that the old destructive introspections and delusions may yet return. The panic became worse and more questions came to the fore. Had Rosie asked Kitty to London in order to discuss her suspicions? This trip – with no planning – seemed so sudden, and this further thought added to the mess already created by my overactive imagination.

I had to stop myself.

I had to speak to stop my mind.

'Whose idea was it?' I asked, as casually as possible.

It had been Rosie's.

I sighed, and realised it had been a large sigh, so I pretended to yawn and proclaimed my tiredness.

No reaction; I mustn't react to her answers.

Had Rosie said anything yet? How would I find out?

Kitty clearly thought the conversation was at an end, and did not elaborate on her reasons for seeing Rosie. I concluded that if distrust was there, she would never let on in any case, and any further questioning would only serve to add to any suspicions she might harbour.

After drawing this conclusion, I realised I would just have to let time unfold, though as before, I took comfort in thinking that Rosie would not upset things unless she was absolutely sure. And she would have to be astute to be so. And so instead, as I lay there after the lights were out and we had said goodnight, Kitty now asleep, my mind began to recall my last meeting with Hannah. It was obvious that she had been brought up as a Christian, and still believed, never having questioned even the smallest of problems with her faith. I didn't blame her. Her father had been a vicar, making any deviations from the norm even harder than it would otherwise have been.

But how could she teach her daughter, aged seven, these crass beliefs about Heaven and Hell? Why had she not ever questioned any of these beliefs before? But progress had been made: she was beginning to question them. Because of me. I hoped the simple questions about an omnipotent, omniscient and omnibenevolent God would intrigue her to learn more. I didn't want to destroy her faith, but I did want to make her think. Perhaps give her some knowledge to question the basics, easily asked, difficult to answer. I did not doubt that her religion was a comfort to her, as it is – undoubtedly – to all believers, but it also struck me that she was a stronger woman than one who needed such a comfort.

Maybe she was realising the same.

How was she reconciling our affair – I didn't like even thinking that word – with her faith? For me it was as easy as it was hard. I loved my wife, and I loved Hannah. I loved my wife more deeply, but I'd never had the attraction with her as I had now with Hannah. Did that mean it was simply lust? No… I had been in lust before, and I would be again. This affair was more than the manifestation of my lust for Hannah, it must be more. Could, therefore, my love for Hannah develop into a deeper love than that I had with my wife?

Philosophy and ethics kept me awake for hours, until I suddenly came to her last question.

Did she think I had not thought about it? Had she devoted as much time to it as I? I wondered how she would have answered it herself.

'What is going to happen between us?' she had asked.

Her

I lay in bed, not able to sleep. I thought, as usual, only of Alex, but now I had asked him – I was pleased to have asked him – the biggest question that lay between us, religion or no religion, I still wanted the answer. I played and replayed the conversation in my head, trying desperately to read Alex's thoughts by analysing his words. His words which I could remember verbatim. His words. I couldn't remember other people's words the way I could remember his.

'What is going to happen between us?' I had asked… I slipped back to the scene as if it was happening again.

He rolled away from me, and picked up his shirt, slipping it on as he sat watching me.

'That's something I wish you hadn't asked. Not yet, anyway,' he said, for him, very seriously.

'Why?' I asked as he did up his shirt. Was that it? Had the end of our affair begun with my question? As each button was fastened, I wondered if that would be the last time I saw his beautiful, broad chest disappearing behind the buttoned shirt. Had I already run my hand across it for the last time?

'I don't want to think about it. I can't think about it. I am happy, now, and when I leave, in fifteen minutes, I'll be miserable. I want things to stay as they are, but I know they can't. Not long term. I'm as confused as you. I love you.'

I would unbutton his shirt again! Happiness flowed into me, and panic left as quickly as it had come.

'I love you too!' I said, leaning over to him once more, and wrapping my arms around him, feeling his biceps protecting me as he did the same.

'I love you so much.'

I smiled, but my face was over his shoulder and he couldn't see it.

'I can feel you smiling,' he said.

God, I loved him!

But I needed to know more about what he thought. My subconscious had already told me that he wouldn't answer now, but without consulting it, or thinking, I had already asked: 'But what *will* we do?'

I don't know,' he said, letting me go and dismounting the

bed, doing up his belt, all the while holding my gaze. He smiled.
'Simple question… impossible answer.'

Coincidence?

Him

And so Kitty went away to London to see Rosie. It was a Saturday, and I knew Edward was away too, though I didn't know where or why. I had been dreaming of spending the night with Hannah since I'd known our spouses would be absent together, and I had already made up my mind to visit Little Cottage in the hope that the dream would be realised.

I knocked on the door.

'Hello,' she said, unenthusiastically.

'Hello,' I said, mimicking her tone. 'Kids here?'

'We're painting. Please go. Even I know that kids are more shrewd than adults. They notice little things.'

I paused,

She was right.

'Go!'

And so I did. There was no arguing with her. She had never spoken to me like that before, and she looked angry in a way I had not seen before. But I departed with a sense of loss and disappointment, and with every step along Henry Lane became more filled with worry and doubt. Had her question about what would happen between us, now spoken, now more real, made her decide she no longer wanted me? Had my answer been too casual, or too non-committed? A simple question with an impossible answer. Had the impossibility of any happy conclusion made up her mind to stop the entire affair? Had she been disappointed that I had not said I loved her and wanted to be with her, despite our marriages? How could I know what she thought when she didn't want to see me.

When would another opportunity like this arise? Would I ever spend a night with her?

I became angry that she put her children before me.

When I arrived home, despite loving and being loved by two women, for the first time since leaving London, the loneliest of cities, I felt alone.

Her

I was cross he'd come again. Edward was away, it was true, and he knew it, and I knew that Kitty was away. I was cross he'd come, but forgave him. I understood why. But I just needed time to think. Time away from Edward and him. Time with my children. Aside from being in his arms, I was happy spending the weekend with Lucy and Harry and watching their delighted faces as we did fun, childlike things together. Things that I used to do with my parents as a girl. Things where men and love had no meaning. It was good they had had no meaning. I needed time to think. As I watched my children splashing daubs of primary-coloured paint over their painting books and the kitchen table, I became fearful for them when they would reach the age where love began to interest them. It saddened me that all might not be happy for them, and that their mother was making such a mess of it in her own life.

Him

When Kitty returned, I was burning with desire, for her, and to hear what had happened. Once the former had been satisfied, which seemed to please her and cheered me to the point where worry was almost banished – she would not behave like this if she thought I had been conducting an affair – I asked her about her weekend.

'How was Rosie?'

They had had a great time, shopping, going out, chatting and gossiping.

The number of bags that Kitty had brought home was evidence

enough that shopping had featured highly on their agenda, but the thought of her chatting and gossiping again brought worry to the forefront of my thoughts. Almost paranoid imaginings whizzed round my head to the extent that I began to wonder if her sexual desire had been a test, to see how I reacted to her amorous advances.

I thought that if indeed it had been a physical probing I had passed it rather well.

After that we fell to talking about Rosie and London and with every sentence that Kitty uttered, I became easier, less troubled. I tried not to ask too many questions, just in case she was leading me into a trap. But as the conversation continued, thoughts like these became less common, and I even began to feel guilty that I was so suspicious of my wife.

Eventually, after I had had a good account of her weekend, Kitty said that she had some sad news.

My heart quickened, a butterfly entered my tummy. Someone had died, or Rosie was heartbroken again.

My thoughts were not allowed to go further, because Kitty spoke again.

I had not imagined what she would say.

She announced that Hannah had been having an affair.

It was as if Thor had used Mjöllnir, his hammer, to smash a foundation stone of our house to smithereens, and the house, my life, seemed to be being destroyed from within. The bed seemed to fall through the floor into the living room where the floor gaped open, almost allowing me to see into the magnificent depths of Valhalla; the walls and beams clattered all around us, destroying the furniture and breaking the windows as they did so, while all the time Odin laughed up at me, drunk at his great table of fallen warriors. But it happened in silence, and after a few moments I realised all was intact, save my nerves.

It had been some years since some such a vision had been so real, and that frightened me too; I could not face a relapse now, on top of everything else. But these images that now came crashing back, more real than ever, and filled my mind with confusion, terror, dread.

In the silence that now reigned, Kitty looked at me.

It was an odd look. Not suspicious exactly, but enquiring. I attempted to expel my guilt to consider what it meant. Enquiring was probably right. She wanted to know what I thought. I mustn't delay my answer but I needed to get it right. A sentence began forming, but my guilt played havoc with it, and I paused again. Odin reprised his laugh, in contempt of my position, but I banished it and silence once again fell.

I felt as if being arrested for a crime I knew I had perpetrated, and that anything I said could and would be taken as evidence against me.

'Bloody hell!' bought me time to say, 'How on earth did you find that out?'

Kitty said that she and Rosie were talking about my birthday, and what a small world it was that Hannah should have arrived, and that she knew Rosie wanted to say something, but was holding back.

'Sisters are very dangerous!' I ventured…

Kitty smiled and said she only knew me better than her sister, and she could tell when Rosie was bursting with confidential information. Rosie had thought it all right to tell her because the affair was over. My musings had not been futile, then. I could tell Kitty was still waiting for my thoughts.

'Things like that happen to the most unlikely candidates,' I said. 'I wonder if she is dreadfully unhappy in her marriage?'

I wondered that an awful lot.

It was the reason why most people committed adultery, after all.

But strangely, it dawned on me that I was very happy in my marriage.

I loved Kitty, and I told her so.

She loved me too.

My heart began to slow.

I asked her what she knew, though of course I already knew the contents of the postcard explaining the end of the affair, and Rosie had not been able to expand on that. They had not spoken again, then. Kitty could only tell me that Hannah had said that she had fallen in love instantly, and about her love for him, for me, had been unlike anything she had experienced before. She had told Rosie that she felt like this was the first time she had fallen in love. She had told Rosie about her first orgasm.

And then as if she had said too much, Kitty announced that she was going to change the subject and then did change the subject. She said that she'd seen Edward in London.

The giant again wielded his hammer in the ruins of our house, but this time the blow came from above, and the roof and beams from above came crashing down for a second time and seemed to hit even me, lying in the bed which had already fallen through to the ground floor.

Had I been so foolish and short-sighted?!

Had Kitty, my Kitty, my trustworthy Kitty been playing the same game as me, with Edward?

Boring Edward?

Had my affair blinded me to hers with him?

An avalanche of thoughts roared through my head in the next couple of seconds. Extreme jealousy and the anger that I discovered accompanied it were prevalent – the initial suffocating deluge of snow and ice – followed by a thousand smaller thoughts and a cloud of anxiety – the powder snow and spindrift: bewildering, annoying, but not fatal.

How would I deal with this?

'What did you do with *him*?' I asked, before I could think.

They had been for a coffee, Kitty said, having met crossing Cavendish Square. She then asked why I had asked in such an extraordinary manner.

'I was surprised that you'd met him, and even more surprised that you'd done something with him.'

Kitty pointed out that I had not known that she had done

anything with him until I had asked, and that my question had been phrased as if I had known that she had.

'I knew you had... your tone of voice suggested that you were about to tell a story...'

She looked at me dubiously, and declared that she had not realised that she had such a tone of voice.

She did not, but her face relaxed, and a hint of a smile sparkled across her eyes. For the first time since she had announced that she had seen Edward, I relaxed. But I chastised myself for speaking and enquiring without thought. Suspicions from such false moves would be easily raised. And she recounted her coffee with him – his idea – and even said that she had not really enjoyed it. She used the adjective *boring* which surprised me; she was usually so polite and not quick to judge or comment badly on others. But the truth was he was, and it was not difficult to come to that conclusion. Why had not Hannah seen the same? Young love, religious love, both disastrous to the wrong people.

Suspicion

Her

Not seeing him while Edward had been away had been good for me at the time – it had allowed me to spend some much needed time with my children and forget about him and Edward – but now no conclusions had been reached and I longed for him again. Lead us not into temptation! How cruel was God to taunt me thus, I thought, swiftly altering my argument to shift the blame to the Devil, only to remember Alex's words and thoughts on this. He must be right. It didn't stack up. God could not be the god I had always thought him to be for any of this to make sense. God's own conduct began to worry me and it seemed that Alex's logic was more logical than God's.

I was now waiting for Alex to arrive whilst thinking about my chance meeting with the vicar that morning. He was an unusual man, but today he had been more unusual than usual. Could it be that he could detect doubts among his flock? I laughed to myself at the thought. It was ridiculous, but how more ridiculous than the rest of my faith? He had asked if everything was all right in my life – a curious thing to ask – as if probing me. How do you tell a vicar – your vicar, and your father's successor to the parish – that you are having doubts about the faith in which you were brought up? His faith?

Then I wondered whether his question had come not from a divine hotline singling out the sheep with ecumenical health problems, but through simple observation. Had he seen me the last time in Church when I had not chanted, for the first time in living memory, what I was supposed to believe? It was true – I had not – I had been thinking too hard about what the words meant, the words themselves, as Alex had taught me.

And then another thought struck me. Could it be that his question did not relate to my religious doubts, but to my marital ones? Had Edward – a close friend of the vicar – been voicing his concerns? Had Edward noticed my unusual behaviour to a degree that was causing him real concern?

Did Edward *know*?

These thoughts sickened me, and I jumped off the kitchen chair, spilling my tea, this time for real.

I paced the room in panic.

I could not know what had induced the vicar to ask if everything was all right in my life. To keep my sanity, I had to conclude that he was just being a little more unusual than usual, or that if it had been inspired by a worry of his, it was a worry founded only on his practical pastoral sense. These were, after all, the most likely and most logical answers, and I hoped my answer would have put pay to his doubts, if indeed he harboured any.

I had, of course, told him that everything was absolutely fine, though I realised half way through saying it that of course *absolutely fine* meant, and sounded, quite the opposite. Would he notice? I hoped not; he was a vicar after all.

But I had lied to him, and gone home, perishing the thought.

And then Alex arrived.

'Darling…' I began, but remembered guiltily that he'd asked me not to call him that.

'I'm glad you called me that,' he smiled.

'You are? I did remember…'

'I know. I saw it in your face.'

How did he know me so well?

'But,' he continued, 'this time I'm pleased. I thought that perhaps after the big question came out before, you might have decided that what was going to happen between us had already happened.'

'I don't know what will happen, or how it will happen,' I said, 'but I don't want it to end yet.'

'Nor me.'

And it didn't, that day.

Him

I was pleased to be going to see Hannah, despite being concerned it would be the last time I did so in my capacity as her lover. It was one of those mornings (I was in one of those moods) when even terrible possibilities seemed all right, and I thanked *someone* and was pleased when en route, Dr Parsons came into view, ambling down Henry Lane, his old-fashioned doctor's bag under one arm. I thought it lovely that such sights, such people, still exist in England. He wouldn't have looked out of place a hundred years ago, save for the lack of a hat.

'Morning! House call?' I asked superfluously, but to begin conversation.

After some unusually friendly and enquiring chitchat, we both carried on, him to continue his round, and me to carry on with Hannah, if she fancied it.

She called me *darling* which pleased me, and we made love.

'Darling?' she said again, again pausing hesitantly and in anticipation of my displeasure after she had done so.

I laughed and then she laughed.

Her

'Yes, dahling?' asked Alex, trying to be entertaining.

'I'm worried about the vicar...'

'Good God! Is he sick?'

'Don't joke... It might be about Edward.'

'Oh...?'

'He asked, "Is everything all right in your life?"'

'A little odd, but he is odd. He's a vicar.'

'A little odd, yes, and I thought he was asking about my faith. Last time I was in church I began thinking about how the service was conducted, about the words we say, and I think he may have noticed me not participating.' Alex looked surprised but said nothing. 'How do you tell a vicar you are having doubts?'

'I didn't know you were.'

'Well… Then he said, "Since I married you and Edward, you have changed," and I became worried that Edward has been talking to him, about his own doubts.'

'What did you say?' asked Alex, shifting position uneasily.

'I told him I was older and that I was now a mother. I said I thought that people never stopped changing. He said he knew I was right, but that I should talk to him if he could help in any way with coping – he used that word – with the changes I was going through.'

'Maybe God told him you were faltering…'

I would have become cross if I hadn't had the same thought. I began to dislike the way Alex made a joke of everything.

'In religion or marriage?'

'Both maybe,' said Alex, casually, but seeing my expression, he continued. 'I suppose you are worried the vicar has been the recipient of a divine enlightenment…' I shook my head, 'which leaves the possibility that he has been *very* observant whilst conducting a church service – a single church service…?' I nodded. 'where you did not behave as you always have – or that Edward has become so suspicious that he has voiced his concerns to the vicar?'

'That was my real worry.'

'I don't believe Edward would do that, even if they are close – they are close, aren't they?'

'Yes.'

'But still I don't believe it. This is not a village of French peasants where the priest is paid to listen to his flock's sordid secrets.'

'You're probably right…'

'Do *you* think Edward would confide in the vicar?'

'Probably not.'

'Don't worry about it, then. Not until you have firm evidence.'

He was so logical, it was difficult to argue.

'You are probably right,' I admitted. 'Thank you.'

He smiled, but the doubt in my mind did not fade.

'But there is more…' I continued.

'With the vicar? You have to tell me everything at once so I can form reasonable conclusions based on the facts!' he said, light-heartedly, but still chastising me a little.

'No, with Edward.'

'Oh.'

'He asked me about his muddy shoes.'

Alex clearly did not understand, and a smile began to form on his lips. It made me cross; it was he that did not see the relevance and not me that was becoming paranoid.

'When you came over, and took your shoes off…' I began.

'But that was weeks ago!'

'He hasn't forgotten.'

'Well, what happened?' he asked urgently. The relevance had become clear; it was not me that was becoming paranoid.

'He asked why I would have been angry because of his muddy shoes.'

'I thought you said he *did* actually have a pair of muddy shoes?'

'They were his walking boots. They were with mine, and mine were just as dirty. But he pointed out they had been like that for weeks.'

'Surely you got out of that one?'

'I laughed it off. I told him I had to scold him for something. I told him I was only joking, and I'd said it only because he looked so sweet and helpless in his ill state.'

'That would have worked with me.'

'I'm not sure it did with him.'

'Why?'

'He didn't look convinced.'

Alex sighed.

'You think I'm worrying over nothing, don't you?' I asked. He nodded. 'Well, you weren't there. There was something not quite right about it. But it gets worse. You know at your birthday when

I said I'd posted Rosie a card?' He nodded. 'Well, last week I did actually try and post some letters – some mine, and some Edward's – in the postbox that I would have to have used to post Rosie's card if I'd done it on the way to your house… and the postbox was boarded up. Edward came home and was cross his letters hadn't gone – we wouldn't get the discount for early payment on something or other – and I said I'd tried, but the postbox was out of action.'

'I don't understand,' said Alex.

'Edward said the postbox had been like that for months.'

'I see.'

'He didn't say anything. He just looked at me to tell me he knew I had lied about Rosie's postcard.'

'Well, surely he thought it was just a white lie to please a friend?'

'There is no such thing as *just* lying. And there is no such thing as a white lie. Edward and I both believe it, and he knows I do too.'

'You did believe it. Do you now?'

'Oh! I don't know! That's another question. But the point is, he thinks I *ought* to believe it, and I wonder if he thinks there is a reason for my newfound immorality in the lying department.'

'How should I know?' said Alex, impatiently.

Why wasn't he being more receptive about my concerns? They were eating away at me, daily, hourly, and I knew that they were founded outside my imagination. Why didn't he suffer as I did?

Him

Her head was filled with doubts. Silly doubts, and paranoid doubts, and I became resentful that she was offloading them on me in order to make them more bearable for herself; I had enough to think about, without her problems too. My brain was so full of guilt and anxiety, and further worry about lapsing back into the my Dark Days of hallucinations and fantastical imaginings, that it felt as though one more woe might cause it to collapse under their combined weight. It felt unfair that she could voice them, while I could not come up with immediate answers. I did not know how the vicar or Edward viewed their questioning, and she knew them infinitely better than I: what did she want me to conclude? How could I comfort her without knowing where their thoughts had originated? I had feelings of guilt too, and doubts, and I wanted her to share my doubts, to feel what I was feeling, to add to her woes, to lessen mine. And so I started:

'Did you know that Edward and Kitty met up in London, for… coffee?'

The shot hit her plum between the eyes, and I could almost see all her previous worries evaporate as she considered the seriousness of my revelation.

'So you didn't know?' I asked, though it was plainly obvious she did not.

'No. Christ.'

She had blasphemed and I wondered what Edward would have thought of that.

'Well,' I said, 'I have quizzed Kitty on it, and I don't think they are having an affair.'

'An affair! I hadn't even thought of that. I assumed they had met up to talk about us! Was it arranged? How long were they together? What did Kitty say?'

And I answered her questions, of which there were many, and told her all I knew of the seemingly innocent, chance meeting of our spouses. Her panic, to my surprise, actually reignited my doubts about the coincidence, but after some minutes discussing it, and after I had reported that Kitty had not seemed in any way different after it, and she had said that Edward (despite his earlier inquisitions) had not either, we concluded it was indeed innocuous. The only odd thing remained that Edward had not told her, but, we argued, perhaps it meant so little to him, he had simply forgotten to do so.

'I concluded,' I said, to reassure both of us, 'that either they were having an affair – which seems preposterous – or that it was chance. Neither of them would arrange to meet each other in London when somewhere more locally would have been far easier.'

'Your logic is worryingly impeccable,' she said.

'If they are suspicious, why would Kitty *tell* me about it?'

'People having affairs cannot help mentioning their lover.'

'Maybe I should mention you more.'

'Why would you do that?'

'I never mention you. Your lack of mention might be suspicious…' The argument went round and round, leading me to conclude: 'We can't win!'

'It worries me that we worry about such little acts of fate.'

'Guilt has that effect,' I said.

And for lack of new avenues, that conversation petered out.

But still I felt as though this revelation had not worried her enough. She had brought up a whole string of doubts, suspicions, and they all rested heavily on me, despite, for now, us both having concluded that they had originated from factors outside our affair.

And then another worry struck me, though I felt cross that Hannah's paranoia was contagious.

At the time I had thought nothing of it, but Hannah's expressions of doubt and fear now ate away inside me: I had remembered the questioning of Dr Parsons as I had passed him earlier, on the way to Little Cottage.

'Dr Parsons…' I began, and Hannah looked at me sharply. Was she also concerned about him? I thought not as her expression became calmer; she was just jumpy, and now seemed relaxed about this new conversation. 'I saw Dr Parsons on the way here. He asked me an odd question…'

'Well…?'

'He asked if we were enjoying village life.'

'What's odd about that?'

'You are right; it wasn't the question that was odd, it was his remarks afterwards. He said he was pleased that we had made so many friends in the village, and said that it was remarkable how close you could get to certain people so quickly.'

'He's a doctor. Like vicars, they have to be good at small talk.'

'We haven't *so* many friends in the village, and the only person I'm close to is you.'

'I see what you mean.'

'And then he said, "This village is wonderfully close knit, which is lovely, but it does mean everyone knows everyone else's business, especially if you happen to be the doctor". And then he winked. Odd, don't you think? But you are probably right, it was just small talk.'

But it did not look like Hannah still held that opinion; she had gone deathly white.

Consequences

Her

I could feel the blood drain from my face. Where did it go? To my stomach? It would need the extra blood, I thought, to form the knot that almost made me double over. Once I'd dispelled this nauseating feeling, I became angry that my physiology should again give me away in such an obvious fashion.

I had hoped not to tell him, but now I knew I must, and with this realisation came the flash of anger that ignited what I knew would be a prolonged rage against Dr Parsons. How dare he talk to Alex like that! Thoughts of formal complaints against him were the immediate manifestation of my anger, though these subsided as I realised they would be futile. But how *dare* he talk to Alex like that!

Alex waited patiently for me to explain myself; he could see something was seriously amiss and I wondered how he could be so patient. How was he feeling? Had he guessed? If it had been me, I would have been shouting at him to tell me! But it was hard. I looked around the bedroom.

On the dressing table stood Edward and I, happily smiling at the camera in our wedding photograph. I had forgotten to take it down and put it in the drawer. The sight of it unleashed an avalanche of guilt that tumbled all around me, silently filling my ears with a cacophony of white noise. I think it must have drained any blood left in my face right down to my toes.

My chest felt hot, but I shivered.

Was this emotional, or did my state cause it?

Him

Though I knew something was amiss, I did not press her to tell me. I had become partially immune to her worries and I was tired of her paranoid mental wanderings; no doubt this would be another. I thought that by being patient, I would be more powerful. Perhaps she would think I knew what she was about to tell me; perhaps she would think I was stronger for not demanding to know immediately. I followed her gaze, her blue eyes looking bluer than normal because of the whiteness of her skin. They were resting on a wedding photograph of her and Edward that was standing on the dressing table. In a moment of idleness, and to distract myself from the other problem, her unspoken problem, I wondered why it hadn't been there before but found no conclusion except the most obvious, that it was always there save when I came.

And then out of the blue she said it.

'I'm pregnant.'

There it was, in all its stark truth.

I did not bother to ask if she was sure; I knew she was, she had two kids, she had been through this before.

Without meaning to, I smiled at how wrong I had been about her obsessive thoughts driven by guilt. This was not paranoia or anything close to it. This was a baby.

'It's not bloody funny,' she said, her body writhing away from me, seemingly at the limit of exasperation.

'Sorry,' I said.

I was, but it was not the time to explain why I had smiled.

Like Christian, her burden must have been huge, and I felt immediately guilty that just a few minutes earlier, I had added to it, intentionally, deliberately.

'I am sorry,' I said, though I did not expect her to guess why.

The enormity of it took a while to penetrate my cognitive thoughts, and when it had, I realised that there was the problem of whose child grew in her womb. I racked my brain trying to think of how early in the pregnancy it was possible to ascertain the father's identity. I knew it was possible, but could Hannah know now? She could not, surely? Amniocentesis, a needle in the amniotic fluid would be required to gather the baby's DNA. But would Hannah do this? Did it matter? The news was still enormous whoever was the father. If Edward was, Hannah would be out of action for months and months, and if I was… I shook my head and exhaled.

She opened her mouth to speak but nothing came out.

'Go on,' I said. 'It can't get much worse!' I was now impatient to hear her.

'Edward's had a vasectomy.'

'Jesus!'

'Don't blaspheme.'

'Why not? This is fucking serious. I've blasphemed before and I've never been struck down by lightning!'

But a bolt of lightning flashed before me. I glanced out of the window, but the sky was clear; I blinked quickly to dispel the fancy, to banish it, and turn my attention back to Hannah. More calm now, I mused that perhaps her pregnancy was evidence that lightning strikes in mysterious ways. But my head began to implode with unanswered questions, though one question surfaced so frequently I realised I had to confront it. Until that moment of clarity, I had forgotten that her admission of pregnancy had stemmed from me talking about the strange words of Dr Parsons.

'What has all this got to do with Dr Parsons?'

'He knows all about it.'

'You didn't tell him I was the father did you?'

'No, of course not.'

'Well what's the problem then?'

'He referred Edward when he had his vasectomy.'

'So he knows Edward isn't the father?'

'That's what I would infer if I were a doctor,' she said, nastily.

'And you think he thinks I'm the father?'

'Don't you?'

The doctor's words came flooding back. He knew my business, all right.

'Yes.'

'That makes me livid,' she said, 'that he talked to you like that.'

'It does me too,' I agreed. 'But isn't he bound by the Hippocratic Oath?'

'He is, but what did he give away? Only a guilty mind would infer anything from his comment.'

She was right, though I was seething at his impudence.

This flurry of peripheral thoughts had led me away from the crucial point, and it was so crucial I still could not quite believe it; I needed confirmation.

'So you are pregnant with my child?'

She did not seem to think this an unreasonable question, and she put her hand on my forearm and nodded.

I sank back, exhausted.

She said nothing. There was little to say, right now.

And I was pleased she said nothing, and did not look as if she wanted to either. She must have known that a moment to think was the best thing.

So I began thinking.

I should be having this baby with Kitty, and it hurt, it more than hurt, it tore my ventricles apart and blood haemorrhaged through my chest at the thought. I could not bear to think what she would think if she knew, the natural mother of my first child. I could not bear the thought any longer.

I thought then of aborting the child – I had never been against the notion – but somehow that did not seem the answer either. This child was mine, and though it grew in Hannah, I felt strangely protective over it. It took me a moment to realise what this new emotion was, but it became obvious: I felt paternal. Paternal. Even the word seemed a misnomer. I was not one to feel paternal! But I did.

Of course the child should be allowed to grow and be born. It would destroy both our marriages, but it would cement my relationship with Hannah, and she, after all, was the woman who had changed me, altered my chemical balance, more than any other. Thoughts of fatherhood sprung to mind, and suddenly my paternal instinct told me that a child now with Hannah, whom I loved, would be worth the heartache caused by its birth.

Maybe Hannah's maternal instinct told her the same. Was abortion even an option? I had no idea what she thought about it, and even if in theory she was in favour, many women cannot do it once the babe has been conceived. Maybe her maternal instinct had already led her to an irrevocable decision.

'Have you told Edward?' I asked, almost casually, thinking she had not, but almost expecting her to say yes.

'Of course not. Don't worry, I won't tell him.'

This is as it should be; it was not his baby, nor his problem, not yet at least.

I smiled at Hannah, I supposed ruefully, but I think it may have been a smile I had never done before. She returned a similar expression.

We both sighed simultaneously.

'Well, what shall we do?' I asked.

A similar question had been asked not so long ago, but now this question encompassed the original one, while gaining so many more facets, that we both knew it was unanswerable at that moment, or even soon, without a great deal of thought.

'We don't have to do anything just now,' she said. 'Let's both think about it for a week and see how we feel then.'

I was pleased with her answer.

Unholy Ghost

Her

It hadn't seemed so bad when Alex had been there – he had remained remarkably cool about it – but now he was gone I felt utterly alone and beyond miserable. The rain which had begun when Alex left had trapped me inside and I felt like a prisoner.

I had no idea what to do. Arguments for and against keeping the baby rattled round my empty head like peppercorns in an almost empty peppermill, grinding them down slowly, the dust falling out of the bottom and disappearing.

In desperation, I almost prayed, but stopped in anger. Would God allow this? How could He? Was this pregnancy the work of the Devil, or his avatar, his beautiful avatar who had entranced me, and whom I loathed at the same time for getting me into this mess. Alex would have asked how could an all-loving, all-powerful God do this, and I asked it now too, finding no sensible answers. Perhaps there was no answer. Perhaps there was no God, and if there was no God, Alex would not be an avatar at all. How stupid of me to think he was in the first place. Then I wondered briefly if God had made me pregnant to punish me for my sins, but the same argument destroyed that possibility.

What would my father have thought?

I wished he was still alive to guide me, but then I wondered whether I would have had the courage to tell him what I had done.

But I knew, in the end, I would.

He would love me, whatever sins I had committed.

And then I thought of his letter.

Though my father had died suddenly of a heart attack, for the last few years of his life, after my mother died, he took to writing my sister and me letters on New Year's Day. They were only to be read after he died, and he kept them with his will, writing a new one each year, and burning the previous year's effort in the fire in his study. He acknowledged it was an odd habit, but my mother had done it for him, and her letter was his most treasured possession.

I had opened mine just after his funeral, and now it was *my* most treasured possession and the only thing I kept from Edward. I had read it hundreds of times, and knew it word for word. But it wasn't that letter that I thought of now. Intriguingly, the letter had come with a smaller envelope within, sealed with wax bearing the stamp from the family signet ring. That envelope was marked, "*Only open this if you are having serious doubts about your faith.*" It had fascinated me for years and I shuddered to think how many hours I had spent awake considering every possibility I could conceive concerning its contents. I had been toying with the idea of opening it for some weeks, but knew this had to be the time. I fetched a sharp knife so as not to spoil the envelope and unzipped it carefully.

The paper slipped out easily, eerily, and I read my father's neat hand.

At Home
New Year's Day
The year of my death

My darling Hannah,

I meant what I said: do not read any further unless you are having serious doubts about your faith. You cannot un-read or forget this, and your perception of me will almost certainly be changed forever.

You will remember my library – full of books about religion and the Bible – but also those many apocryphal tomes on genetics, evolution, palaeontology and the history of religion. I read them initially to understand more, to convince me that science and religion were not mutually exclusive. In the end I concluded that they did not have to be, simply because religion requires a blind belief. But the more I read, the more I doubted that God could exist as we have believed. The great religions were born when humanity was infinitely more ignorant about the Earth and the Universe than we are now, and virtually all the fundamental beliefs of Christianity cannot be believed by an educated, rational mind. So my doubts about God became a certainty that Christianity is nothing more than a moral code for leading a good life. Christ was a great man, but he was only a man, and worshipping a mortal is clearly daft. I then came to think of God not as himself, but as a presence in the Universe, but eventually was forced to abandon this idea too. Evidence is the key, my darling. Always think about evidence.

The evidence I found made me a devout atheist, and I'm proud of that. I have deliberately not set out what I learned here – that is for you my darling – if you choose so to do. But you are bright and I hope you have kept some of my books!

I'm proud of what I learned, and that what I learned in the last ten years of my life overturned what I had believed – and believed with all my heart – for the previous fifty years. But do not for one moment think that I regret going into the Church. I had a long and happy time as vicar, and my joy of helping people, spiritually or otherwise, keeps me more than satisfied when I think of it.

You will wonder why I did not tell you.

First, for the Church. I love the institution of the Church (if that is not too nonsensical!) and the last thing they need is their priests losing their faith. Enough people do that without encouragement. Second, for your mother. You will understand, no doubt! Third, and perhaps most selfishly, for you and your sister. The Vicarage was a splendid place for you two to grow up (and I rather liked living there too!). Simple as that.

But the Christian ethics are sound (though the vast majority predate Christ). My advice about how to live your life is in the other letter, but if I were alive, it would make me proud if you lived this life (your only one) well. Love and allow yourself to be loved. Be kind to others and forgive their trespasses as we used to pray. Forgive me for leaving you this letter when we cannot talk of it, now or in heaven, *for I do not believe we will meet there (and if I'm wrong, I'll be downstairs anyway!).*

I am your father, and, I fear, an unholy ghost, but always,
Your loving,
Daddy

P.S. I'd rather you didn't tell your sister (she has the same sealed letter) but I will leave it to your better judgement. If you want to know if she's already read hers, ask her "Whatever happened to Daddy's signet ring?" in those words.

P.P.S. I'm wearing the signet ring.

Only my father could make me laugh from beyond the grave in this gravest of situations! How I longed for him. How I loved him! I always thought that the love for my husband would surpass any other, but blood is stronger. I loved him, and my mother, and my children far more, and that moment was the first time I'd ever consciously had that thought.

And then the enormity of his words struck me.

My father, the devout vicar, had died an atheist.

Lightning Strikes

Him

When I left Little Cottage, the sky was dark. Low, grey clouds scudded beneath a huge cumulonimbus, towering up into the heavens, black and foreboding. Somehow a shaft of sunlight had found its way through the leaden sky and illuminated the fresh, glistening grass, a glorious bright green; but more remarkable was the lighter, fresher, more spring-like colour of the sunlight striking two trees that were just bursting into life after their autumnal abscission and long wintry wait, contrasting magnificently with the black stormclouds above.

It looked like a portal into Odin's Asgard.

But no, I must not let the phantasmagoria take hold again; banish it.

As I reached the end of Henry Lane, the first spots of rain began splatting around me, causing the two men working at the side of the road to leave their labours, donning their coats and running for shelter in the cab of their little open-backed lorry. It was only when they had departed that I saw what they had been doing. The sign of Henry Lane looked like new: the rusty welts had been sanded away, and the background had been painted a brilliant white. They had almost finished the black lettering, and only the last 'e' remained unpainted. And the vegetation round the sign had been cleared: the ivy had gone, and the only evidence it had ever been there was a couple of newly sawn stumps at the base of the wall. A cement trowel lay on a board of almost finished cement; most had already been used to re-point the wall.

I was pleased that they had re-used the old cast iron sign, rather than replacing it with a cheaper, less pretty, modern alternative, and I hoped the rain would not spoil the fresh paint.

As I passed the little lorry, there was a tremendous flash of lightning, itself not visible, but lighting up the clouds from behind, turning them a brilliant white for its duration. A tremendous thunderclap followed almost immediately.

Had Thor descended from Asgard?

A terrified dog, not Benji this time, ran along the wall, cowering, tail between its legs, and in through an open gate of someone's front garden. I wondered whether, if I had let Benji find his own way home on the night I had met Hannah, events would have unfolded as they had. I would have met her, it was a small village, but would the manner of our meeting have been so electrifying? We would never know.

And then I wondered whether fate had led Benji, and then Hannah, into my arms. Fate? A peculiar concept, and empty without an accompanying belief of something more powerful, a religion, a belief in God.

And then it struck me that God might have sent Benji, a messenger, leading me to Hannah. The thought did not last long, and I cursed myself for having it. It was ridiculous; I had looked down on Hannah for her belief, the one major flaw in her character. I had even tried not exactly to dispel it from her mind, but certainly to make her consider its validity, and now here I was having religious thoughts myself.

But what was fate, without something more powerful behind it?

I decided not to follow this dog, whether sent by God or not: I could not cope with more turmoil, more decisions.

And anyway, I concluded, it seemed to know its way home.

I continued walking, skirting the edge of the village where houses met fields, in order to take in the natural beauty of the countryside and impending storm. As I passed an electricity pole, a tremendous flash accompanied by a massive ripping sound scared me rigid; a fraction of a second later came a huge, deep boom, seemingly part of the ripping sound, but emanating from deep within the bosom of the clouds above. I had never heard lightning whilst seeing it, and knew it must be upon me.

In my fear I cowered from the electricity pole. Had the lightning hit it? It was not on fire, and I remembered a picture from one of my childhood books of a primitive man staring wide-eyed in terror at a tree that had been hit by lightning, now on fire, the man believing that the wrath of the gods manifested itself in these great displays of natural power. Terror struck my heart, and I knew I must get away from the electricity pole. I quickened my pace, but could not move my eyes from the top of it, though it was now just behind me. Would this tall conductor attract the lightning, and if so, would it jump across to me?

Not being able to rip my eyes from it, partly in horror, partly because I wanted to see the bolt of lightning that killed me, I slipped off the edge of the pavement and fell, twisting as I did so to keep the electricity pole in sight. I landed on the road, my hands subconsciously extending behind me to soften the fall, grazing my palms.

The electricity pole still held my terrified gaze, and I was rooted in the position in which I had fallen.

I prayed.

I prayed to God to forgive me, and not to take me just yet.

And the lightning struck again.

It was hard to know whether the flash or rumble came first, though I knew that physically the flash must have done, and it was hard to know whether the bright fork came from the heavens and hit the electricity pole, or whether it shot upwards from the vertex of the pole. The speed with which my senses took in the light and sound confused or tricked my brain, and they did so again as the deep, low boom – that seemed to stem from the initial ripping sound of the lightning but somehow also preceded it – rang out.

I knew that I had not been hit by the lightning. I knew because as soon as the flash of lightning had gone, I saw the electric cable detach itself from the top of its pole. Its detachment happened in slow motion, and once free from its tethering, the wire began to fall, snaking itself wildly as it did so. It hit the road next to me, and continued to writhe, almost making me believe it was alive. It seemed to take hours, though it can only have been a second, but finally it came to rest almost touching my hand.

I stared at it and knew a slight movement of either hand could be the end of me.

But I couldn't move.

It may have been a minute, maybe longer, before I gradually shifted my weight from the hand, and then the hand away from the wire, very slowly at first, but finally whipping it away.

As I finally breathed relief, another flash of lightning lit up the clouds from within, and I desperately recoiled from the wire; but this time there was a discernable delay between it and the thunderclap that followed, and I knew I was safe.

I praised God, actually uttering the words, 'Thank you.'

And then the heavens opened.

Within a minute I was soaked. Normally this would have made me cross; I dislike a soaking intensely. But on this occasion, I loved it, the feel of the cool water on my shoulders, and head. My face was dripping, but my shirtsleeves were so wet that wiping it made no difference. I felt as though the water was cleansing me, physically, from being in contact with Hannah, but more deeply too. I felt as though each drop was washing away one of the dreadful sins I had committed over the last few months, and after a while, I felt a great weight lift from me. Though they had undoubtedly been sins, they were so natural and so right that I knew that now I was being forgiven for them.

I felt baptised.

Rivulets of water ran over and between my fingers: my hands were still on the road, propping my torso up in the direction of the electricity pole. The dead snake of the electric cable was still inches away. I felt very self-conscious and looked around to see if anyone had seen me, grovelling on the road next to a broken cable.

Apparently they hadn't, and I stood up, soaking, trembling. But alive.

I picked myself up, and gazed up at the pole. I supposed the heat of the lightning had caused the wire to fall, and I turned, my eyes following the dead python along the road to where it began rising, up to the next electricity pole. There was little I could do with it, and the thought of touching it horrified me. With my whole body shuddering, I began my walk home again.

Just then the front door of one of the houses opposite opening, and a cross-looking woman emerged. She looked at me, somewhat sceptically, but with less hatred than she might have looked on a half-drowned rat. She then scrutinised the broken cable on the road and complained bitterly that the bloody phone lines were down again, just when she had been chatting to her son. With that she went inside, slamming the door in anger behind her.

Revelation

Her

Not wishing to malinger at home in a state of despair, it wasn't long before I had scoured our bookcases for the books my father had left me. I had previously thought many would remain unread – I had kept them because they had been my father's – but now I made a pile of them with the intent to devour as many as I could as quickly as I could. I began to read.

Him

At home, and still rather dazed, though I was now warm and dry, I lay on my bed and stared at the ceiling.

The jagged shape of the lightning bolt against the dark sky, the black electricity pole and the terrible wire serpent that had loosed itself as the bolt had struck were still vivid in my memory. But the lightning had not arched to me; the serpent had missed my hand by less than a finger's length: I was still alive.

These thoughts, and my previous confusions, worries and guilt ran in ever-decreasing circles through my mind, which eventually could not cope with all their ambiguous and contradictory messages. It became too much. The thoughts became so bewildering that they melted together into one frenzy of confusion that overtook my brain, allowing it no further thought as a kind panic rose within me.

But as I lay there, I discovered that my brain began again to function, if only to replay my memories: my whole life since meeting Hannah flashed before me, in reverse order, far too quickly for me to consider each episode, but without missing one.

This vividly electrifying series of visions ended at the beginning, with the rasping whisper of a rocket clearing the rooftops and thousands of tiny stars radiating from its subsequent explosion like the beginning of the universe, and then sound of quadrupedal pawsteps belonging to a dog called Benji. And once this film reel of the preceding six months had rewound, once I'd reached the beginning, last November, my brain seemed to clear entirely. My pulse slowed and the rising tide of panic and hysteria fell away like the waves on a stormy lake dissipate as an immediate calm descends; the shrouds of doubt were lifted from the dark tomb of my mind that had until now been blind; my confusion dissolved into joy, and it all became so obvious.

My life had been guided by God.

Everything fell into place: from the beginning, it had been planned; it was God who had sent Benji to me, the rocket our guiding star, and so to Hannah; it was He who had allowed us to fall in love instantly, at first sight, deeply, unbelievably; it was He who had called me to Church, through Hannah; it was He who had allowed our love to flourish beyond even the strength it had from its moment of inception; it was He who had thwarted attempts by the Devil to disclose our love to others; He had allowed our union, and so our destinies were bound, in my own eyes, and His; it was He who had kept Hannah's faith strong in the face of my misguided preaching; it was He who had blessed me, and Hannah, with our child, a child which I suddenly, and with a wild certainty, knew should come into this world, its parents united; it was He who had dispensed lightning to show me finally His physical strength and power, and once done, it was also He who saved my life from the electric serpent, so that I may live in the knowledge of Him and in the newness of life.

Why had it taken so much?

Why had I not seen before?

But of course it did not matter; that too had been part of His plan: I had been stubborn in the presumed faith of my own knowledge, but once an obstinate mind yields, once that being *believes*, so it is ready to be sowed with knowledge and faith anew.

That week I did little else but read. Though the enormous burden of the baby loomed somewhere in the depths of my being, my father's words, and the words of his books burnt themselves into my conscious. I began to think that in order to solve the huge, seemingly insurmountable problem of the baby, I must read, I must learn, to become less ignorant. Edward thought me very strange, suddenly burning with this desire to read these books in which I'd previously had no interest. But I concluded that however things turned out, I should tell him of my father's letter, so I did. He would need an explanation, and this was truly it, though I didn't tell him the full contents of the letter. I simply told him I had to read these books, as my father wished me to. The full truth of me having doubts about my faith could, if necessary, be explained in full. But not now.

I read about many topics and learned that the whole world of knowledge that I had been dimly aware of was in fact much more advanced and widely accepted that I'd previously acknowledged.

I read about who wrote the Bible, when they wrote it, and how accurate it might be; about the theological problems of heaven and hell, and how an omnipotent, all-loving God allows evil and suffering; about what happens to those righteous unbelievers, or those who have never have a chance of finding God through Jesus; about Christianity's affinity, or lack of it, to other world religions; about creationism versus evolution, culminating in its most striking aspect: human evolution. The idea that we had evolved from monkeys had horrified me, but I'd also known that the theory had not been proved. That elusive evidence, or many pieces of evidence, the *Missing Link*, was still lacking in our knowledge, and without it the scientists still could not prove that humans had indeed evolved, and were not made by God in his image.

But I found that it was a myth. Hundreds of missing links had been found and described; people knew when these half apes, half humans lived; they knew where they lived, how they migrated, and how they evolved into new species after they had found new homelands to inhabit; there were whole family trees explaining the relationship of one species to another; there were pictures of each species showing clearly the transformation from quadrupedal, arboreal apes into bipedal, upright forms, much more closely resembling man; they were given long Latin names, culminating in the most advanced genus, *Homo*, many of these species being almost akin to modern man, that unique species, *Homo sapiens*, but a species of hominid nevertheless. How anyone could think that man was different to or above other animals astonished me in light of my newfound knowledge, and I felt utterly ignorant, blind and stupid for once believing that we could be.

There was no *Missing Link*; even the phrase was redundant in my mind, and it struck me that anyone who argued for it must be ignorant, as I had been. And I found my father had thought the same: his annotations throughout these tomes all pointing to the conclusions he'd so concisely penned in his letter.

I felt as if I had been blind, and my father and his books had undone the mask across my eyes.

Him

On the day I had found God, I had prayed for the first time since I had been a boy. I had asked for forgiveness, for Him to forgive my blindness, my doubt, and for Him to forgive all those multitude of trespasses that had until now been unforgiven, me having been an unbeliever.

And as that week progressed, I began finding comfort and solace from having found God, knowing that he had forgiven me, and my prayers were becoming more frequent as my relationship with Him deepened. For the first time in my life, I felt truly happy within myself, without the need of another mortal to provide that happiness.

All my cares dissipated in the wind as I knew His decisions were what mattered. All I had to do was follow His path. He would show me the way.

It was easy.

And now I knew that God had planned for Hannah to conceive the baby she held in her womb, I knew that have it we must, whilst bearing the consequences. I knew that she had more to lose than me, already having children, but, I concluded, she wouldn't actually *lose* them. Certainly, we would both lose our spouses, but we would gain each other, as I had gained God.

I wondered what Hannah was thinking about the baby, though in my heart, I knew she would want to keep it. She was a mother of two; she would not, she could not, kill another child, already growing inside her. Our religion would keep her strong and give me strength to support her. God would not allow her to destroy the child. Besides, I was the father, and she loved me. She loved me more than her flaccid husband, and I loved her more than Kitty.

Despite this certainty, I longed to see her, though it was still days until we had planned to meet again. I longed to see her so that we could make our decision together, and work out how to execute it once it was made.

Her

Later in the week a letter arrived bearing Rosie's handwriting. Immediately I was thrown into a panic. She did send postcards from her regular travel destinations, but never letters, and I wondered what she felt needed the protection of an envelope.

I tore the letter open, and read:

London
Monday before Easter

Dear Hannah,

I've been meaning to write since your postcard and since we saw each other at Alex's birthday. What a coincidence you should end up in the same village! But I'm pleased you have, and that you have met.

I'm glad things have worked themselves out for you. I was worried for you when you said you were having extra-marital thoughts. It is good that he's now out of mind and sight, and I hope everything with Edward and the kids is back to normal. How lucky you were that things didn't get more complicated.

I've just had an abortion (don't tell Kitty, she'd never forgive me). The father didn't want to know me after I told him I was pregnant and in any case the decision was easy. I had been rather keen on him but once I knew I was pregnant the thought of having his child filled me with horror and revulsion. Funny how something like that brings you to your senses. I feel free and liberated. It's probably bad of me but I don't feel sorry at all.

Anyway, I started seeing a new chap. He's a Christian, which is all very odd, but apart from that he's so perfect! He does have some peculiar ideas, though. I hope he sees the light soon, because I don't think I could marry him as he is. Do you think I should give up straight away? I'm no theologian, but I must say I do find it hard to understand how anyone can believe in god in this day and age!

Well that's my news! I suppose both pieces will seem fairly momentous coming out of the blue but I don't feel much troubled by either.

Let me know when you're next in London and I'll let you know when I'm going to visit my sister again. Happy Easter!

Love from

Rosie x

Dear Rosie! She did make everything so straightforward, and I envied her way of thinking. I was relieved at the letter's contents: here was firm evidence that any suspicions she harboured about my affair were clearly long gone and I felt almost honoured that she trusted me with news of her own abortion. It amused me that she wrote so candidly about her new Christian man, and his peculiar ideas, not realising that until very recently, I had wholeheartedly shared them. Had my faith been so private she had never known? In some circles, perhaps; I had never been an evangelist. Had she ever known I was a vicar's daughter? She had never met my father, and I felt a tang of guilt for not ever having told her more of him. I smiled wryly as a re-read her words on abortion, as if such a terrible thing would or could not happen to me.

Dear Rosie, so wrongly innocent!

But what amazed me most was Rosie's ability to sum up so simply one thought that my subconscious must have already had, while not sharing it with my conscious self. I had already decided that the child that grew inside me must not be born, and though there were many good reasons for this – my marriage, my children, my husband and our decision not have any more children, my own, old desire to have only a boy and a girl, thankfully already realised – I perceived that the main, overarching and strongest reason for not having this child was that I was now filled with fear at the thought of it being Alex's.

Last Blows

Him

We had agreed to meet the following Friday, Good Friday, as it happened. Edward, thankfully, was making the most of the bank holiday, and had taken his children, their children, on a day trip; Kitty too was making good use of her time and was in London for a friend's going away party. I was not sure who the friend was or where she was going, but it meant Kitty was away, and that was all that mattered.

Normally, I would have looked upon it as good fortune that the bank holiday had come then. Without it, the long Easter holiday would have kept Hannah's children at home, and me away. But now I viewed it with renewed interest as it was Good Friday. It was the day of Christ's crucifixion, and I wondered whether God had another message for me. Even if He did not, I knew the importance of the day, and had decided that it was important in my life partly because of its intrinsic significance in the Christian calendar, and partly because of its significance in my life. Upon this day might be made life changing and wonderful decisions, and I set off for Little Cottage in high spirits, especially because I was looking forward to telling Hannah about the revelations I had received since I had last seen her. I knew the smile she would give me as I told her: it would say *I told you I was right*, before breaking into her smile of happiness. I knew she would be happy that God had spoken to me.

Her

I was dreading his arrival. I knew that whatever his thoughts on the baby, this would be the last time I wanted to see him.

Since reading my father's letter, and then some of his books, I had made up my mind entirely. Rosie's letter cemented that decision. Alex was no avatar of the Devil, I saw that plainly, but he may as well as have been. I became angry with myself for not having thought more clearly about what might happen before things had begun with him. I suppose I knew deep down that whatever happened would bring disaster. After all, how else could an affair end? I felt a fool for ever starting it.

I had no idea what Alex had been thinking since I last saw him. Perhaps I had nothing to worry about. I knew that many men fled from pregnancies, and maybe he would welcome my decision to have an abortion. But he'd been so cool about it on his last visit. And not only that: he had been acting oddly, and this worried me.

I was dreading his arrival, but I could only wait.

Him

Turning into Henry Lane I saw again the new, white road sign, clear of ivy and looking very proud, but before I had time to contemplate it further, I saw the almost familiar figure of Dr Parsons walking towards me. He greeted me cheerily, as he usually did, and asked if I was just out for a stroll.

'Yes, just out for a stroll,' I replied, my heckles already raised by his inquisitive question, which I know knew was based on the suspicion, or perhaps even belief that I was the father of the babe he knew Hannah carried.

'It's a lovely day for it,' I continued, almost with the intent of deepening his suspicion.

Though no thunderstorm or black cumulonimbus clouds lurked, it was not a lovely day, and he peered up at the monotonous grey sky. He agreed with me, and it amused me he was so easily led.

'I was rather hoping to bump into you,' I said, leading him to ask why.

'After your comment last time, I wondered if you had any

gossip to share,' I said.

This put him on the back foot, quite literally: he stepped back with a nervous smile and laughed it off. He even went as far as saying that he had meant nothing by his last comment and that he hoped I hadn't taken it the wrong way.

'Oh, goodness, no,' I said, 'How could I possibly?'

His smile became a little more relaxed before he declared he must go in order not to be late for his next appointment. I detested the little man for thinking he could act as some minor god, using his confidential, professional knowledge of people to make loose remarks to folk he hardly knew when he no business to do so. But I wasn't going to let him have the satisfaction of knowing this.

'Cheerio,' I said cheerily, pleased that I had been able to pay him back for his previous indiscretion, but also sorry and repentant that I treated him in such a manner. I had no doubt that I would have behaved as he had done had our positions been swapped. But, I argued, no real harm had been done, and I had treated him as I would have expected him to treat me.

And so onwards to Little Cottage.

Her

I opened the door to see Alex looking very cheery. It would have pleased me better to see him grim, contemplative, in light of our combined mess.

He tried to kiss me on the lips, but I pulled away.

'Not today, Alex. We have important things to discuss.'

'But I haven't seen you for over a week...' he started, stopping only when he withdrew from me and saw my serious, worried face.

'Sorry,' he said, 'you are right: we should talk first.'

There wasn't going to be anything after the talking, though.

'Come through. Coffee?'

And so we sat in the kitchen. This was the first time we had begun one of our meetings there, and I wished that more of them had started similarly. I still felt like I hardly knew him, and again I became cross that I had allowed our relationship to spiral out of control whilst we were so ignorant about each other.

'Have you been thinking?' he asked.

'Of course I have.'

'That's not really what I was asking. Have you reached a conclusion?'

'Yes.'

'Good. Me too,' he announced, and opened his mouth, apparently with the intent to tell me his.

'Go on…' I said.

'I want you to be the mother of my child. I want to be the father of your child. I want you.'

It was as if the whole kitchen had become a vacuum, and that vacuum extended inside my head. I knew I was there, I could see the kitchen table, our mugs of steaming coffee, but my peripheral vision seemed to open up and suddenly the room became much larger, and everything in it smaller. I could suddenly see details about the room that were familiar, yet seemingly unnoticed previously: Harry's painting of the house pinned on the wall, with far too few windows, its roof a lurid orange; a string of garlic bulbs hanging by the cooker; the clock's painted face with its crooked second hand, ticking silently, its mechanism, or my aural faculties, not transmitting its sound in this vacuum; a thousand other little details.

And then it was as if I was looking on the scene as an observer. I could see a woman sitting opposite a man, and I knew one had said something momentous to the other, and that one was in a state of shock, wondering what to say. And then I realised that the woman was me, and my perception brought the scene back to that woman's eyes, my eyes, as suddenly as it had departed from them in the first place, and I sat staring at Alex, still without any idea what I should say next.

'I don't know whether you look surprised, pleased, or displeased…' he said eventually, after one or two nervous shifts of position that I processed only after he'd spoken.

'I'm afraid I wasn't thinking very much.'

'Which means you are surprised,' he surmised.

'Yes, I suppose so.'

'Well, is that a good thing or a bad thing?' he asked, impatiently.

I knew I had to tell him my mind had been made, but how?

The easiest way:

'I want an abortion. Our affair cannot last. I love Edward, and my children, and I want things to stay as they are.'

Him

I had not expected this in a million years, but it was perfectly obvious why she was against the idea: she presumed me still to be a heathen, and I knew that once she knew God had spoken to me, and that I had listened, she would change her mind. She had chosen Edward over me because he had God. Edward, the husband whose love was nothing like that which I could give her.

Her

He sat with an odd expression, his eyes fixed on mine. I thought perhaps he was accepting his fate, and would break into a wry smile before saying goodbye and making an honourable departure.

But a smile didn't follow, and instead he leaned forward, very seriously, and in rather an intimidating manner.

'I have something to tell you,' he said, 'that I think will change your mind.'

And with that, much to my relief, he leant back and waited for my reaction, which I didn't give him immediately. He clearly didn't know me well enough: once I had considered something – and I had spent the last week doing little else – and once my mind was made, I was resolute and stubborn in the extreme. I pitied his self-assuredness, his belief that he could or would change my mind, and I let my face show it. But he hadn't seen me express pity before, and I don't believe he understood my expression.

'I'm sorry, Alex,' I said. 'I've already made up my mind.'

'I will change it.'

'Alex –'

'No. Let me change it.' We both paused, but he thought of what to say first. 'I know that our religious differences have been a problem from a start. I'm sorry I tried to make you doubt. Well, actually, I didn't try and make you doubt, I just tried to make you think. I'm glad your faith was strong enough, but I have been thinking too. I thought so much that I began to believe that *I* was wrong.'

I had no idea where he was going with this circuitous and somewhat rambling spewing forth of ideas, but so quick and excited was his speech, I couldn't think of a way of stopping him. So after a pause, which was, I believe, to let me interrupt, he carried on:

'You see… and this isn't easy for me to say after everything I've said before… God has spoken to me, and I now I believe.'

One of my eyebrows raised itself quite by mistake.

'You don't believe me? I'm not just saying this to convince you here and now. I will tell you all about it in due course, but don't you see? It makes everything so much easier!' I didn't see how it did. 'I know you don't want me because I lacked faith, but now I have it!'

His eyes gleamed so bright, and his voice was different, full of an eerie enthusiasm. I did believe him: my reaction had been surprise, not disbelief. But there was something in his manner that scared me. Though in many ways we were still strangers, I knew enough about the workings of Alex's mind to know that this was not the reasoned reaction from the logical, scientifically versed man of even a couple of weeks ago.

I needed to know more.

'Why the sudden change of heart?' I asked.

His eyes gleamed more brightly. I think he thought he was in the process of changing my mind about my decision.

'Do you now want to know how it happened?' he asked.

With all my heart no! I cursed myself for even asking a

question. This man, this man whom I had invited into my home, and my body, was becoming rapidly unhinged, and as he did so, he became frightening as well. I began to wish he would leave. Not just the house, my life, but the village, the county even. My skin began to crawl at the sight of him...

But I couldn't bring myself to say no.

He explained, hurriedly, excitedly that he now knew that God had wanted Benji to lead him to me, that God had made me for him, and him for me. He asked how else could we explain the instant and total attraction? As his words kept coming, it became apparent that he was in earnest: he obviously believed that God had allowed me to become pregnant, and as he explained his experience in the thunderstorm, I realised he truly thought that God had finally proved his existence with lightning and serpents of electric wire.

He's lost his mind, I thought, a flicker of amusement passing me as I realised only a month ago he would have considered me to have lost mine – or of never having had one – for my belief in God. But why had his sanity seemingly been spirited away? Had Kitty found out? Had he burnt his boats at home, pushing him into a desperate attempt to make me his? He believed, all right. Could emotional distress cause an atheist to believe in such short order? His evidence was ludicrous! Coincidences and a lucky escape in a storm! Nothing more... Did he even know that it had been the telephones and not the electricity that had been out that afternoon? If his serpent had hit him, he would have been bruised, not electrocuted.

My scepticism must have been apparent, because, apparently somewhat hurt, he asked:

'I thought you'd be pleased I have found God.'

'I'm not sure if I should be pleased that you have found God.'

'Why not?'

I wanted to explain everything: my father's letter, my newfound knowledge, my decision – years ago – not to have more children, my love of Edward, my conclusion that the affair would and could end only in heartbreak. But so big were these thoughts, I had no idea where to begin.

So instead, I concluded the simple answer was the best:

'Your newfound faith – and I do believe you – has no bearing on my decision. I'm sorry, Alex.'

He looked down at his chest as if I'd just plunged a dagger into his heart and was just contemplating his last few moments of life.

He looked up at his murderer, and with a terrifying look, asked:

'You're sorry? Is that all I get?'

'I can say it again if you want.'

He shrugged off my answer.

'So you have definitely decided?' he asked.

'Yes.'

'Despite my faith?'

'Yes.'

'Have you seen Dr Parsons about it?'

'Yes.'

This seemed to answer another question that he hadn't asked. Words again failed me, but I could see his mind whirring.

'I know we have sinned,' he said, 'but God has forgiven our trespasses. I have been baptised, and He will do the same to you too. God has blessed us with this child,' he continued, his passion rising. 'He has blessed us with each other. I love you.'

His eyebrows had arched themselves into a worried, pitiful look, and pity filled me also, together with worry. Worry for how his mind had been altered, so radically, so quickly. I held his arm, feeling his muscles which would in the past have caused me to rip off his shirt. Now I could acknowledge he had fine arms, but his shirt remained in place.

'I was in love with you, too,' I admitted. 'Once... In a way.'

'Are you trying to differentiate being in love and love itself?'

I supposed I was, though remembering what I'd whispered in his ear even a fortnight ago, I felt a little ashamed.

My silence answered his question.

'They are just words,' he said. 'We knew how we feel. And I

still feel it.'

I couldn't argue with him, of course. But I had come to my senses. I knew that two marriages and the happiness of my children were at stake. I knew that the end of two marriages would break the hearts of four adults and infect two tiny, child's hearts, with the truth of infidelity and a lack of trust in marriage and love forever.

His senses seemed to have left him; he had considered of none of this.

I had to let him know how I felt now.

'I knew how I felt, but it isn't how I feel now,' I started. 'I know I love Edward, and my children.'

'But there is a third child. Do you not love that one, though unborn, as much?'

I hadn't; it had been his.

I realised then that I loathed him in his new guise – he seemed almost unhinged – and as a result, I loathed the creature that had grown inside me because it was his.

'I'm sorry.'

'Stop apologising!' He rose to his feet, impassioned, though thankfully, he came no closer. 'If you were truly sorry you would ask God for forgiveness, and you would see he would send you a sign that we needed to be together. He *must* have planned it. Are you so blind?'

'Why are you so sure?'

He didn't answer immediately, but looked at me, pity in his eyes. Pity, I presumed, for me not seeing God's plan.

'Why,' he began, 'are *you* so sure? You, who have been sure about God all your life…'

'Even I know that becoming pregnant is a biological function,' I said, beginning to become angry.

He too looked vexed. 'God has blessed us with this child. You must know that. And now the Devil has taken hold of your soul, putting evil thoughts there. Aborting this child would be evil, you understand *that* surely?'

'No, I do not agree.'

He huffed like a belligerent child.

It was impossible. The conversation had reached a natural conclusion. He did not agree with me, or I with him, but the irony was that if I'd never met him, I might once have done. He still stood, but he had calmed down now, and I think even he realised we had reached a stalemate.

'So…' he started again, this time, to my relief, much more calmly. 'You don't want the child and you won't want me? And I cannot change your mind?'

I nodded.

'You will change your mind,' he said, confidently, arrogantly.

I knew then that I must stop his wild delusions.

'There is no child any longer.'

That stopped him dead.

'The evil has been done?'

His sinister words shocked me, but I remained calm and nodded.

'My love for you,' I continued, 'died before our child.'

I couldn't believe I had uttered those words, so cruel, so heartless. But Alex was a different man, a man who had seemingly lost his cool logic, and with it, his sense of reality. I could think of no other way to tell him that his altered mind might accept.

And it seemed to work.

'I see,' he said.

He sank back in the chair, smaller, more feeble than I'd ever seen him, and I wondered whether I had broken him, or whether he'd broken himself.

'Will you be in Church on Sunday?' he asked, finally.

I nodded.

'See you then, then,' he said, and plucked his coat off the back of the chair, departing immediately, but not before turning at the kitchen door and smiling so calmly and kindly that it unnerved me for several days afterwards.

'Goodbye,' he said, and let himself out.

No Doubt About Edward

Her

Relief is not strong enough a word to describe how I felt when he left. His behaviour, his words, had frightened me, and I even bolted the front door after his departure.

I was worried that he had become so unbalanced he might tell Kitty everything, or worse still, Edward. His last words worried me. He knew we would all be in Church. It was, after all, Easter Sunday, and though the day had less meaning for me now than it ever had done before, for the sake of my family I could not absent myself. What was he planning to do? I could find no rational explanation in what had just been said, or what might happen, and I was too emotionally drained to try.

It was a joyous moment when Edward and the children, all three of their faces glowing with happiness, returned home that evening. It was lovely having some normality back in the house. Their presence put these questions to the back of my mind, where I kept them intentionally locked. The questions would still be there tomorrow, and on Sunday, but there was little I could to answer them do in the meantime.

That evening Edward and I were lying in bed, him reading, as usual, and me lying with my chest pressed closely to his side, my feet tucked beneath the arches of his, thinking, as usual, my arm around his chest, helping to support his book. I was happy here, in my bed, in our bed, safely with my husband. I gave him a little squeeze and he wiggled his toes in return. I smiled.

After a while, I became aware that Edward was no longer reading, but staring at something in the room.

He asked where our wedding photo was.

'I was dusting, darling,' I lied, cursing myself for having to do so, yet again.

He looked down at me, and I pretended to be uninterested, hoping that he would not be able to feel the quickening of my heartbeat on his chest. He asked where it was.

'In the top drawer.'

He extricated himself from under my arm and walked across to the chest of drawers, opening the top drawer and promptly pointing out that the frame was hidden under some shirts.

'I put the washing away. I was in a rush, darling.'

He pointed out he'd ironed those very shirts last weekend.

'I was just rearranging.'

He drew a finger along the chest of drawers where the photo stood, and without words, showed me his finger. Along the inside edge was a thick layer of fluffy grey dust. It was the lack of words that scared me: he had announced his growing suspicion silently.

Edward's obvious suspicion terrified me. Would everything unravel even now, after the conclusion of my sins? The irony was that Alex hadn't even been into the bedroom on that occasion. I had moved the picture only as precaution, in case in a moment of weakness, we had just one last moment together. But that moment had thankfully been avoided; not even the desire had been there. I had been strong, and Alex had left unsatisfied in every regard.

'Bugger,' I said, to his surprise. 'Must have forgotten to dust the top, darling.'

He thought me very odd, which for a moment, in my guilt, I thought was his way of vocalising his distrust, but he smiled and declared that now the kids were out of my hair for most of the day, I had too much time at home, and that perhaps I should go back to work.

I smiled.

'You are probably right, darling. You know how particular about things I normally am!'

His smile broadened, and he got back into bed, kissing my

forehead fondly.

'And that, darling,' he said, 'is one of the reasons I love you so much!'

'I love you too, darling, so very much!'

And we settled back into the pillows, under the covers, close, my arms wrapping him up tightly. I knew that if Edward had harboured any suspicions they were now set aside. Perhaps it was only my guilt that led me to believe he'd even been doubtful. I didn't care. I knew I loved him, and he me.

Words from my father's letter came to mind. *Love, and let yourself be loved.*

I smiled again. My father was right, in so many ways.

My eyes swivelled in their sockets to look at Edward. His book was in the way, obscuring his face, and with my free hand, I gently pulled it down so I could see him.

'Hello!' he said, and I crept up his chest, kissing him when I was close enough.

He kissed me.

We made love.

We made love and then we fucked. It was wonderful!

Edward and I, as far as I could remember, hadn't fucked like that before. It was better than anything I'd done with Alex, perhaps not in the rawest, physical sense, but because as we gazed into each other's eyes, I knew that I truly loved Edward.

Afterwards, as we sank back into the pillows, Edward's eyes twinkled in the way only his did, and I knew he was going to crack a joke.

'Bloody hell, have you been practising?!' he said.

Easter Sunday

Him

On Easter Sunday, Kitty and I set off for church, though she had required some persuasion.

I had, of course, been thinking deeply about my last meeting with Hannah, so much so, that on more than one occasion, as I had been staring into space, or pacing this room or that, Kitty had asked me if I was all right.

'Yes, Kitty,' I had said.

And once my conclusions were drawn, once my pacing stopped, I was all right.

I knew that Hannah had killed our child, and I feared she was full of evil. I knew that God had asked me once more to try and save her, and it troubled me that I might fail.

But I knew that in the end, it would not matter what I could do on this earth. Me failing to save Hannah would also be part of His plan. I could see that she had helped bring me to Him, and once done, He considered her role in my life over, for the time being, at least. There would be time, in the future, for Him to save her. Perhaps she needed this time of darkness to make the light, once she'd found it again, all the more bright. I had faith that her faith would blossom once more.

And I knew, with a rising excitement, that He had other plans for me. And as we went through the Lych Gate and into the churchyard, my excitement rose. I knew I must ask Hannah just once more whether her mind was made, and accept her answer on behalf of God. I knew He would grant us an opportunity to speak, away from the ears of our spouses and local physicians.

I was excited because I was going to Church.

Her

I entered the Church warily, still worried about Alex's behaviour, and what he might do or say. We were early: only a few people had arrived, despite it being Easter, and he wasn't among them. I had brought some flowers for my father, as I did every Easter, and went to the side of the Church where I knew there would a little vase waiting to receive them, greeting some of the aged congregation as I went. The little bunch of wild flowers looked pretty, and I was pleased. Normally, I would be pleased because I imagined my father looking down at them, and I knew it would please him, but now I was pleased simply because they looked pretty. I hoped some of the other members of the congregation would notice them and think so too, and then I felt rather guilty for picking them: perhaps more people would have enjoyed them if they had remained on the little bank beneath the wall of the churchyard where I had gathered them. Still, it was too late.

I turned to rejoin my family and beheld Alex, only two feet away. 'Morning,' he said, quite happily, as if nothing had happened between us, and thankfully, without that odd gleam that had been present in his eye at our last meeting.

'Morning,' I said, a little suspiciously.

He did not seem to recognise the suspicion in his voice, and he drew a little closer. As he did so, Kitty emerged into my line of sight from behind his shoulder, sitting on a pew a few rows back. Our eyes met, and she waved cheerfully. He had not told her, then. I waved back and tried my best to return the cheery smile.

'I just wondered if you have changed your mind?' he asked, quite softly and calmly.

'I'm afraid not.'

'This is your final decision?'

I nodded.

His eyes closed as he dipped his head in acknowledgement. He raised his head slowly, but not quite to its previous position so that it was still a little depressed, and he said, 'Goodbye, then,' before turning quickly on his heel to join Kitty in her pew. I went back to my pew, behind his. As I sat, he turned, and waved cheerfully at Edward from across the church.

I supposed that was it. Relief again hit me, and I felt almost joyous. He seemed to accept my decision with grace and humility, and did not seem unduly heartbroken.

Had it been so easy?

Him

She had put a knife through my heart at my last meeting and now she twisted it. She twisted it with the same force, the same spite, with which she must have twisted her own thoughts. How could she so easily shun God whom I had only found so recently? The Devil played with irony, his evil tool, and I could see that he had her in his grasp, and I could see that she was lost; there was nothing further I could do. I began to pray for her, to God, asking Him to forgive her for her trespasses, asking Him to banish the Devil from her mind. Her future now lay in His hands.

Kitty, next to me, asked me what I was doing.

'Praying,' I said, to her obvious astonishment.

But thankfully, she could ask no more questions because the vicar had emerged from the vestry, and was waiting for silence.

The Vicar

'Good morning, everyone. And welcome to you all, especially on this fine spring morning with which God has blessed us on this day, this Easter Day, the most important day in the year for all Christians. Today is the day Jesus rose from the dead to save us from our sins. He ascended into heaven, where he is seated at the right hand of our Father...'

Her

The vicar's words had a new meaning for me now. He droned on, paraphrasing the same thing every priest all over Christendom would be saying, and had said, year after and year, and would continue to say, year after year. Did he know what he was saying?

Did he believe it? Was he, like my father, saying it because he had to? Because, like my father, he was too weak to admit that he had been wrong? Was he saying it because he was comfortable in the vicarage? Because he loved the institution of the Church? Or was he just ignorant?

Him

The service had begun: I was pleased to be there on this triumphant day. The day Christ had shown the world his power, God's power, as God had shown me in the week before. This was no coincidence. By a terrible show of His force, He was reminding me that He had sacrificed His own, His only, son, for me, for all mankind, and that mortality on this earth was common to all.

Her

'*Alleluia! Christ is risen,*' said the vicar, opening the service, '*He is risen indeed. Alleluia!*' chanted back the congregation, blindly, without a thought.

The Vicar	Her	Him
'*Almighty God, to whom all hearts are open, all desires known, and from whom no secrets are hidden... cleanse the thoughts of our hearts by the inspiration of your Holy Spirit, that we may perfectly love you, and worthily magnify your holy name...*'	You may know my desires; they are honourable, but my heart is closed to you, ineffectual deity... I have never seen your holy spirit. The only spirit that has spoken to me has been my father's, and it was unholy, but wise, full of knowledge, proof.	My heart is open! I have no secrets from you! Just from Kitty, but you understand, she should not suffer... Thank you for showing me the light, the lightning, through the power of your Holy Spirit. I do love you; I will worthily magnify your holy name.

Her

The service continued, and I listened intently to the Bible readings, the words of the vicar, and the words of the hymns. They all seemed empty.

The Vicar

'Please sit for the Sermon.'

Her

Even the word *Sermon* filled me suddenly with dread. I realised that for all the years of listening to sermons, even those my father had given, I had learned virtually nothing about God, or religion, or Christianity, compared to that which I'd learned from just a few of my father's books even in the last week.

Big issues, big, sweeping questions that now filled my mind with every word of the Anglican service remained unanswered, unasked, in fact. The vicar simply took it all to be true, and on the rare occasions that the word *proof* was used, I heard it and remembered it not as proof in the scientific sense, the logical sense, but an illogical demand on one's intellect: to simply *believe*. That was the problem of this religion to which I had previously subscribed. Blind faith was required, and this was seen by this member of the clergy as proof. But as I had learned, I had found that even a little knowledge of science, of history, of Christianity, was enough to destroy any such faith.

I wondered why my father, in his sermons, hadn't addressed the questions I knew he must have read about, but I supposed the answer was clear: he couldn't have done without concluding that his religion had got it all wrong.

My thoughts occupied most of the Sermon; though from the snippets I concentrated on, I knew I had missed only a rehash of last year's Easter preach.

The sheep rose on their hind feet to chant the Nicene Creed.

'*We believe in one God, the Father, the almighty, maker of heaven and earth…*' they began. But how many did? How many, if they read even the most basic scientific literature would shun the fact that the universe is fourteen billion years old, and the earth more than four, and how would they reconcile this with Genesis, or Christian teaching since? '...*For our sake he was crucified under Pontius Pilate...*'

For our sake? This was the one of the fundamental points of Christianity, but such an unnecessarily convoluted and obscure doctrine I wondered why on earth the early Christians had ever come up with it? And when had they come up with it? It was not, as far as I could remember in the Gospels... Had it been instigated at Nicaea? It was the Nicene Creed, after all... But that was over three hundred years since Christ's death.

My ignorance infuriated me; I needed to read more.

'*On the third day he rose again in accordance with the scriptures...*' In accordance with the scriptures: but who wrote them? Men. And when? Which ones? I now knew some of those answers, but still so little! '*...he ascended into heaven and is seated at the right hand of the father...*' I wondered again if the current vicar had thought about what he was saying, or whether years of repeating the same words had numbed his intellect into complete submission.

'*He will come again in glory to judge the living and the dead...*' continued the vicar, leading his flock, '*...and his kingdom will have no end.*'

His kingdom ended where I began.

Him

The words made sense; it all made sense. I spoke them loud and clear, ignoring Kitty turning her head towards me, questioning my newfound enthusiasm. She did not understand, she probably never would, but there was little I could or would do about it. Between sentences, I asked God to forgive her, and to take her when it was her turn to leave the world.

'*We acknowledge one baptism for the forgiveness of sins...*' For the first time, I thanked God that my parents had brought me up a Christian, and that I was baptised. And I rejoiced to think that

God had baptised me again, just a few days ago, on the same day I had discovered that he had blessed me with a child before the Devil had taken it from me. I asked God to forgive the child's mother, to take her when it was her turn to leave the world. '*We look for the resurrection of the dead, and the life of the world to come.*'

I did indeed; I knew that God would want me in His kingdom.

The Vicar
'*God so loved the world that he gave his only Son Jesus Christ to save us from our sins, to be our advocate in heaven, and to bring us to eternal life… Let us confess our sins.*'

The Congregation
'*We have sinned against you and against our fellow men, in thought and word and deed, through negligence, through our own deliberate fault. We are truly sorry…*'

Her
All this was true, though I wanted only Edward's forgiveness. Something I hoped he would never be able to give, because he would never know why I needed it.

Him
Again, I asked Him to forgive me, and more importantly, Hannah. I asked Him to forgive her for the murder of our child.

The Congregation
'*For the sake of your Son Jesus Christ, who died for us…*'

Her
He died for us? But I had asked this question before: now I was considering our supposed beliefs, it struck me – though I couldn't believe I hadn't thought of it before – that even in this single service, the same words, the same phrases had been used multiple times, cropping up again and again in different forms; it was as

if the constant repeating, the constant chanting of the same lines would drum in the ideas, the doctrines, so well that eventually anyone would believe them. It struck me that the draftsmen who had written the service must have considered this. It might, by the sceptical, be called brainwashing, and I wondered whether the writers had deliberately written it thus.

We all, including me, for old habits aren't quickly set aside, said, '*Amen*.'

The Vicar
'Please stand to sing hymn number four-two-eight, *Thine Be The Glory*.'

The Congregation (singing)
'*Thine be the glory, risen, conquering Son; endless is the victory, thou o'er death hast won…*'

Her
But what proof is there? How do people believe, unless blindly?

And so the organ ground on, Martin the decrepit organist becoming slower each week. Sometimes, I wondered whether he'd give out half way through a hymn and topple from the organ loft, tumbling on the less enthusiastic members of the congregation who thought themselves safe in the back pews. This thought had often presented itself, and I often banished it for fear of being un-Christian, but now, I allowed myself a smile.

The Congregation	Her	Him
'…*Let the Church with gladness… Hymns of triumph sing; for her Lord now liveth, death hath lost its sting…*'	Why should we be glad? What is there to triumph over? My father's death still stings me.	God has triumphed! He is alive, and I am too, with Him. Death *has* lost its sting.

Her

The Eucharistic Prayer fascinated me. All the notions we had already chanted and in which we were supposed to believe were reinforced by the vicar in his long soliloquy before the breaking of the bread. It was interesting how the parts of the service that contain the central beliefs of Christianity, or that are meant to be particularly holy, are full of words like *power*, *glory* and *majesty* to rouse the Christian soldiers into stirring belief. Clever writing, I thought.

The Vicar

'*Therefore with angels and archangels, and with all the company of heaven, we proclaim your great and glorious name, for ever praising you and saying…*'

The Congregation

'*Holy, holy holy, Lord, God of power and might, heaven and earth are full of your glory. Hosanna in the highest!*'

Her

I smiled as we knelt to pray the Lord's Prayer, and suddenly the words, '*Hallowed be thy name,*' came to mind; I knew they would be spoken shortly, but I thought of the phrase before the prayer began because of the archaic use of *Hallowed*.

I reflected that God's name was indeed hallowed: but did He deserve it? Did He even exist?

The Vicar

'Please kneel for the Lord's Prayer.'

Her

Who wrote the Lord's prayer? And when?

Him

I knelt, and prayed, and He listened.

The Vicar

'Our Father, who art in heaven,

'Hallowed be thy name.

'Thy kingdom come, thy will be done,

'On earth as it is in heaven.

'Give us this day our daily bread.

'And forgive us our trespasses as we forgive those who trespass against us.

'And lead us not into temptation, but deliver us from evil.

'For thine is the kingdom, the power and the glory, for ever and ever.

Amen.'

Her

You are not in heaven. My own father didn't believe it, and nor do I. My own father is not in heaven.

I can see you now, Daddy, decaying in a pit not fifty yards away, your skeletal crown adorned by the little hair you had left, your signet ring rattling on your bony finger, your skeletal teeth laughing at the afterlife.

Forgive me my dear Edward; I do not need anyone else's forgiveness. Your power and glory has died for me, for ever.

Him

I will see you in heaven, Father.

Your will be done, as you know it will be, as you have told me; I am ready to play my part.

Forgive me, as I forgive Hannah; she knows not what she does!

Banish the Devil from her misguided soul! You have already saved me from temptation, but deliver me safely, when the time comes.

I will rejoice to see your kingdom, your power and your glory.

Amen.

Her

And so the bread was broken, and we ate the body of Christ, and drank his blood, and said our thanks for so doing. A Transylvanian castle and its bloodthirsty inhabitants sprang to mind, and I was pleased that I was not a Catholic and required to believe that the sweet, sickly, communion wine was actually the blood of Christ.

The thought made me smile like a naughty schoolgirl, but only

Jesus, nailed to the limestone cross above the alter, saw me.

And now, with the end of service in sight, I wanted to leave. I wanted to leave to get away from Alex; I wanted to leave because I felt like a hypocrite being here; though my faith had been destroyed, it still felt wrong to be cynical about it in God's house. But as soon as that phrase had entered my head, I hated it: it was like all those other religious phrases that roll of the tongue so easily once said often and regularly: the draftsmen had been good!

Once the whole flock had been fed and watered, the vicar limbered up for the Grace, which surprisingly he had to read, though he must have said it countless times.

And so to the Dismissal.

The Vicar
'*Go in peace to love and serve the Lord.*'

The Congregation
'*In the name of Christ, Amen.*'

Him
I do go in peace, and I will serve you, as you have asked.

Her
For the first time that I could remember, I said nothing.

The vicar caught my eye, and through his blink, I understood that he had understood I had said nothing on purpose.

I wondered whether he would ever try and talk to me about it, or whether he would simply accept that he had lost another of his flock. After all, it was no more complicated than that.

As we rose to leave, I thought it ironic that Alex had shown me the light. God had never listened to me and he was not in heaven. My father wasn't in heaven either.

He was just dead.

Had he wasted his life, preaching hopes and dreams, nothing

more? I wouldn't go to church again. Now I just had to explain why I had lost my faith to Edward, without breaking his heart.

Him

As the service ended, I knew I was a new man; through Hannah I had found something wonderful, something I knew to be true, but which had thus far played a cursory, not even peripheral role in my life; but now, as the bright sunlight entered the church through the brightly coloured windows, it had entered my heart, and uplifted it; I had found God.

Her

The church door was opened allowing shafts of brilliant spring sunlight to flood the church. The vicar, blinking, began to say goodbye to his congregation. Alex and Kitty had reached the door before us; I was pleased that we wouldn't have to talk; it didn't feel right, not today, anyway. Alex smiled sweetly at the vicar, shook his hand and left, following Kitty who had preceded him. As he went through the door into the bright sunlight, he turned. The brightness of the light outside behind his head made it difficult to see his face: the halo of light had made his head almost a silhouette, but I could see his features and the whites of his eyes just well enough to catch the quick smile he gave me.

I forgave him, as I had been taught, not for any religious reason, but simply because it felt right, morally right. I did not understand what particular turmoil was running through his mind, but I knew his soul was far from at rest. And that was the last look he gave me before leaving the church.

Hannah's Epilogue

Her

It happened on the Monday a week after. I like to believe it wasn't suicide. I like to believe it wasn't suicide because it upsets me that a man who once had such a hold over me could have done that to himself so easily. So easily, and so irrationally, for a man who had found God, or even for one who had simply lost his mind.

I don't suppose anyone will ever really know, and that is probably for the best.

Life returned to normal very quickly after Alex's death. Having so quickly rid myself of the physical burden within me, and as the weeks went by, I found that I slipped into forgetting him and the guilt associated with him.

Perhaps this was proof that my feelings for him were not those of love at all. But if not, what?

Certainly, there was magic between us.

But it was short-term, destructive magic.

Perhaps destructive enough to make an intelligent, balanced man become quite the opposite, perhaps unhinged enough to take his own life. That thought scared me.

Certainly, though, Kitty believed his death was an accident. Only a couple of days after it, I passed their house, a sale sign already up in the front garden, and I saw her, and she me, through her kitchen window, crying into the washing up. She waved me in, trying to smile, which dispelled my vague doubt that she knew I had been her husband's lover. We chatted. She was moving back to London, to move in with Rosie. She would be all right, especially with her loving sister, and perhaps better off without Alex anyway. She was young enough to find love again, and beautiful. That was the only occasion I shed tears in relation to Alex's death, and they were for Kitty, not him.

His funeral was in London, but I did not go.